BOWIE HIGH
LIBRARY MEDIA CENTER

P9-BZI-470

Advance Praise for L. Divine and the DRAMA HIGH Series

"Move over *Sweet Valley High* and *Gossip Girls*. *Drama High* has it all—cute boys, backstabbers, and a smart, tough-as-nails heroine that all girls can look up to. *Drama High* is fun, fast and highly addictive. L. Divine writes authentic, compelling fiction. Once you start reading, you won't be able to stop. L. Divine creates a strong, inspiring heroine in Jayd, whose life is anything but simple. *Drama High* offers a rare mix of compelling, authentic and fast-paced storytelling."

—Cara Lockwood, bestselling author of *I Do (But I Don't)* and *Wuthering High: A Bard Academy Novel*

"Following Jayd was so exciting. She was such a true, down-to-earth person. In many of the scenes I found a little of myself in Jayd. The drama she stayed in led to so much anticipation that it was hard to put the book down. This was a great start for the Drama High series."

—Ashley Freeman, Tucker High School, Tucker, Georgia

"When I was reading the book I didn't expect some of the things to happen that did. That's why I really liked it. I'm waiting for the other book to come, so I can see what happens next. I really liked this book because nowadays girls think that you have to give your body to keep the boy, and that really isn't true and this book is an example. More girls need to read this book. L. Divine did a great job. Keep up the good work."

—Bianca Edwards, age 17, Glen Burnie, Maryland

BONE HIGH SCHOOL
LIBRARY MEDIA CENTER

"With such limited options for African American teenagers, *Drama High: The Fight* is a refreshing addition to teenage fiction. L. Divine did a wonderful job capturing the true essence of real teenagers and their life experiences. I read the book in two days. Can't wait to share this new series with the many teens I know who are seeking age-appropriate reading material."

—Lisa R. Johnson, Sistahs On the Reading Edge Book Club

"L. Divine is a brilliant author. Her novel *Drama High* captures the imagination and keeps the reader wanting to turn the page to see what happens next."

—Candice Sewell, age 12, South Holland, Illinois

"L. Divine's novel *Drama High: The Fight* was awesome. Drama High is just like most of the schools everywhere. Every school has characters just like South Bay High a.k.a. Drama High. For instance Jayd, the chill-and-laid-back chick that has no problem saying what she feels; Misty, the school's yap mouth and drama maker; and KJ the school's hottie and athlete that everyone wants to be with.

When I continued reading the book I realized that Drama High is a lot like my school. They both have so much in common. From the Caucasian population and even down to the "imma-whoop-your-butt-for-messing-with-my-man" scenario. That's why every girl should read this book. So that they can put themselves in Jayd's position and learn how to take the mature and reasonable way out of any situation, physical or verbal. Thank you for giving me the opportunity to read *Drama High: The Fight*. I can't wait to read the next two novels."

—Tirsheia Spriggs, age 15, Glen Burnie, Maryland

BOWIE HIGH SCHOOL
LIBRARY MEDIA CENTER

Drama High, Vol. 3

JAYD'S LEGACY

L. Divine

Dafina Books for Young Readers
KENSINGTON PUBLISHING CORP.
http://www.kensingtonbooks.com

DAFINA BOOKS are published by

Kensington Publishing Corp.
850 Third Avenue
New York, NY 10022

Copyright © 2007 by L. Divine

All rights reserved. No part of this book may be reproduced in any form or by any means without the prior written consent of the Publisher, excepting brief quotes used in reviews.

All Kensington titles, imprints and distributed lines are available at special quantity discounts for bulk purchases for sales promotion, premiums, fund-raising, educational or institutional use.

Special book excerpts or customized printings can also be created to fit specific needs. For details, write or phone the office of the Kensington Special Sales Manager: Kensington Publishing Corp., 850 Third Avenue, New York, NY 10022. Attn. Special Sales Department. Phone: 1-800-221-2647.

Dafina Books and the Dafina logo Reg. U.S. Pat. & TM Off.

ISBN-13: 978-0-7582-1637-3
ISBN-10: 0-7582-1637-8

First Kensington Trade Paperback Printing: February 2007
10 9 8 7 6

Printed in the United States of America

Dedication

To my Ori; my grandmother Dorothy Jean; my mother, Dorothy Lynette; my Yeye, Iya Songo Eniola Kalimara, Sharron Robinson, Enola Gay, Omidayo Rochelle, Sheila Hite, Jane Demian, Sheila Rollins, Lana Brown, Theresa Ross, Mrs. Kirkwood, Mrs. Moore, Natam Laurent, Grace Hall, Toni Crowe, Khisna Griffin, Valerie Roane, and to all of the other powerful women's legacies in the making. Keep on keeping on. . . .

Prologue

The smell of freshly cut grass permeates the crisp night air. The crowd is cheering loudly and my heart's beating fast. I don't know why, but I feel like something's about to go down.

As I get up from the bleachers and start walking toward the football field, the coronation has already begun. The parade of fancy cars starts to cross the football field, each carrying candidates for homecoming queen and princess. Nellie's sitting in the passenger side of Chance's classic Chevy Nova, looking like a queen with the Drama Club's other candidates seated in the back. As the cars stop in the center of the field, Nellie's car is second in line and very close to the people in the bleachers.

I come down the bleachers as quickly as I can, trying to reach Nellie and Chance. But it seems with every step I take I'm farther and farther away from the scene.

As Chance gets out of his car to let the ladies out, three people in hooded jackets rush the football field, causing a stir. As Nellie steps out of the car, three people step out from under the bleachers and take out what appear to be big water guns from underneath their jackets and attack Nellie at full force. It turns out that they're not water guns but paintball guns. Chance, trying to protect Nellie, leaps in front of her but gets taken out by the gunman instead.

"Jayd," Bryan says, peeking his head through the bedroom door. "Get up or you're going to miss your bus, sleeping ugly," he says before slinking back to the bathroom, leaving me to worry about my dream. I hope I'm way off on this one because Nellie's too excited about being the first Black homecoming princess for South Bay High.

"Did you hear your uncle? Get up, girl," Mama says. I jump at the sound of her voice.

"Alright, Mama, I'm up," I say, stumbling out of my bed toward the door. Bryan has been picking up early shifts to make more money. I hate when he beats me to the bathroom. It's never a good start to my morning.

"Don't forget about your homework for me, it's due tonight, Jayd. I'll be waiting for you when you get home," Mama says from beneath the covers.

"OK, Mama. I'll see you when I get home," I say. As I head into Daddy's room to retrieve my morning necessities, Bryan opens the bathroom door and cuts in front of me.

"Excuse me," he says, practically pushing me out of his way.

"It's a little late for that now," I say, referring to the stench he's left for me in the bathroom.

"Just thought I'd freshen it up for you before your morning shower, Queen Jayd," he says, reaching up to the top bunk where he sleeps and grabbing his deodorant from under the pillow.

"Next time please don't do me any favors," I say as I locate my toiletries in one of my oversize Hefty garbage bags in the cramped closet, before leaving Bryan to his morning routine. I don't have time to deal with his bull today. After Jeremy dropped me off at the bus stop last night, he made a point to tell me that from now on he would be picking me up from the bus stop in the mornings when I reach South Bay. I want to look extra cute this morning, being that it's our first official day as a couple at Drama High. I'll worry about Nellie later. As with all my dreams, it'll come to pass one way or another. I just hope I can learn to control them sooner than later with Mama's guidance. Until then, I'm just going to go with the flow and enjoy my man and my friend's turn at catching a little drama of her own.

~ 1 ~
New Territory

"In the middle of the madness/
Hold on."

—SADE

I love Jeremy's new habit of picking me up at the bus stop by school every morning. Last night while driving me back to Mama's, he insisted on starting this morning and I don't mind at all. It'll give my feet a well-deserved rest and keeps me from dealing with the uncomfortable stares of the neighbors. It also gives me a few private moments with my baby before the impending drama of the days begins. After last night's dream, I can only imagine what's coming our way.

"Nellie doesn't know what she's getting herself into," Jeremy says, practically shouting over the loud music as we slowly cruise toward campus.

"I know. I told her to be careful. These folks around here will smile in your face and be all happy for her publicly. But, when the shit hits the fan, they'll scatter like roaches," I say, recalling my personal moment of betrayal when I first joined the Associated Student Body.

"Ooh. Sounds like a sore spot. I'm intrigued," Jeremy says. The base from Jeremy's car is so smooth, the people walking around outside with their spoiled dogs can't even complain about the loud reggae bumping from his speakers. He turns down the volume slightly, ready for my story. I readjust myself, straightening out my red Apple Bottom cuffed Capri jeans and matching red shirt as I turn to face him.

"It's not funny," I say, playfully socking him on the arm. "It was a very painful experience, having the entire Associated Student Body ostracize me for speaking up against the favoritism the cheerleaders, athletes, and ASB members receive during the monthly student senate meeting." Almost veering off the road, Jeremy looks at me, shocked.

"When did this happen?!" he exclaims, almost laughing. I'm not surprised he doesn't know. Mickey and Nellie wouldn't have known about it either if they weren't my friends. The athletes and cheerleaders are a tight-lipped clique, even when they're hating. I guess it's bad for their rep if they air their dirty laundry around school.

"Last spring. And, it's not funny," I say, again socking him in the arm, this time a little harder. "I was really hurt when they all turned on me."

"I'm sorry I laughed. It's just I don't understand why you would join an organization and then speak out about the perks, especially during a meeting where the principal and teacher sponsor are present. But, I've got to give it to you, baby. You've got guts. So, then what happened?" Jeremy asks as he slows down in front of the main parking lot, really interested in my story.

"I resigned and joined the Drama Club," I say. "I was already enrolled in the class and played Lady Macbeth in the drama festival. So, I already knew everyone."

"It just goes to show you how ridiculous these people are up here. Nellie doesn't even know what she's getting herself into, especially running against ASB."

"I'm with you one hundred percent, baby. I know how these cliques up here work and I'd never run for anything just because I know how vicious they can get," Jeremy says as we join the long line of cars waiting to get into the parking lot. The first bell hasn't rung yet and students are already hanging out all over the place.

"Has she ever run for anything before?"

"Not that I know of," I say, not really sure. She went to another high school for freshman year, just like me and Mickey. So, I don't know much about her life before South Bay High.

"Well, the competition ain't pretty. During homecoming week, the opposition can be very dirty," Jeremy says, finally pulling into a parking spot and barely missing a squirrel.

"Jeremy, did you see that poor squirrel?" I ask, reaching into the backseat for our backpacks.

"Poor squirrel? You mean that oversize, rabies-infected rat?" he says, grinning at my sensitivity toward small animals. I can't even stand to kill a roach, let alone a small animal. It gives me the creeps.

"Well I'm just a damn riot to you this morning, ain't I?" I ask, stepping out of his ride. As if I hadn't said a word, Jeremy takes my hand and backpack in one quick motion.

"Did I mention how good you look in those jeans?" he asks, eyeing my goodies like he wants to take a bite right now.

"No, you didn't. But, I can tell by the look on your face you meant to." And, he's right. These are my favorite pair of jeans. They fit perfectly and feel good, just like the two of us together.

"Not that I need to remind you, but you always look good, girl. I'm glad you stopped being so stubborn and decided to take me up on my offer," Jeremy says, slipping his arms around my waist and pinning me up against his Mustang. He kisses me softly and makes me forget all about the squirrel. I could stay here all day, but the school day calls.

"Come on, Jeremy," I mutter in between pecks. "I have to catch up with my girls before the bell rings."

"OK, just one more kiss," he says, pulling me in closer. I

wish we could ditch class. His kisses are so worth the unexcused absence in Spanish.

"OK, you two. Break it up," Chance shouts from the top of the stairs leading from the parking lot to campus, completely ruining our flow. "There are young, impressionable minds here. Keep it moving," he says, gesturing his arms like a traffic control officer, drawing even more attention from the nosy onlookers all around.

"Don't you have other happy couples to harass?" Jeremy asks, wrapping his right arm around my shoulders and leading me toward campus.

"Yeah, Chance. Can't you see we're busy?" I ask.

"Jayd, you're never too busy for your boy," Chance says, kissing me on the cheek and falling into step with me and Jeremy while the other students rush past. "And, did I hear you say couple?" he asks.

"Yes, which means no more free kisses," Jeremy says, pulling me slightly away from Chance.

"Hey, just because you're my man don't mean my cheeks, or any other part of my body for that matter, belong to you," I retort, as sassy as ever. I do like Jeremy's newfound possessiveness. It's kind of sexy, as long as he doesn't get too carried away.

"Hey, dude," Matt says as he and Seth walk up to us. "Chance, Jayd."

"What's up, dude," Chance says, giving Matt and Seth dap.

"Well, don't you two make a picture-perfect couple?" Seth says as Jeremy and I stop and lean up against the bicycle racks next to the science building.

"How's Nellie handling the nomination?" Matt asks.

"I think she'll be fine," Chance says, looking around the buzzing campus. "Do you know if she's here yet?" he asks, taking his cell phone out of his pocket and flipping it open to check the time.

"No, but I'm about to find out," I say. "I have to get to my locker before the bell rings. I'm sure I'll catch up with her then," I say, reluctantly rising from my comfortable position next to Jeremy.

"Could you please tell her we need to talk?" Chance says. "She needs to know how to handle the nomination, know what I mean?"

"Yeah. Tell her we've got her back if any shit goes down," Matt says.

"Yeah, I can't wait until Reid gets wind of our nomination. He's going to be so pissed," Seth says, looking like he's been waiting for this moment all his life.

"Why did y'all nominate Nellie?" I ask. I hope it doesn't sound like I'm hating because I'm not. Why they're now her personal cheerleaders is what I don't get.

"Honestly, Jayd, we think she can win. She has that princess quality about her that gives her the competitive edge necessary for full domination," Matt says. It sounds like he gave this a lot of thought.

"And also, she's just enough of a bitch to instill fear in all the other candidates, which is exactly what we need to win," Seth adds.

"Don't be calling my woman a bitch," Chance says, punching Seth in the chest. I knew he had a thing for Nellie.

"Your woman? Did I miss something?" Matt says.

"Nah, you didn't miss nothing. My boy's just got it bad for Nellie and she could care less," Jeremy says, rising from his spot on the bike rack to walk me to my locker.

"I'll relay all the messages," I say, instinctively taking Jeremy's hand and leading him up the walkway toward the Main Hall.

"I'll catch up with y'all later," Jeremy says, leaving his crew behind.

"Later, you two," Chance says. "And, tell Nellie if she needs anything at all, hit me up." Poor Chance. He's picked the wrong Black girl to have a crush on. Although, I think it would be cute if he and Nellie became a couple. Then, we could all hang out together and start our own crew. But, I'm sure Mickey would have a serious problem with that. She's already not feeling hangin' out with the White side of campus. If Nellie crossed over, she'd be liable to leave us both behind.

When we reach my locker, Nellie and Mickey are already there waiting for me to arrive.

"Hey, girl. What took y'all so long? The bell's about to ring and we haven't even had a chance to catch up," Nellie says, reaching out to give me a hug.

"Sorry. It was my fault. We ran into my friends, a.k.a. your fan club," Jeremy says.

"Her fan club? What are you talking about?" Mickey asks. She's already on the phone with her man, I assume, and I'm sure they just saw each other. He comes to her house every morning before he goes to work, bringing her fresh dough-nuts from Randy's Doughnut Shop. They are too cute.

"Chance, Matt and Seth are looking for you. They want to give you some pointers on being the Drama Club's nominee for homecoming princess, with the first round of voting tak-ing place at lunch and all," I say.

"Oh, that's so sweet," Nellie says, twirling strands of her hair around her index finger; she must have gotten a fresh perm this weekend. "I'll have to catch up with them at lunch."

"Voting? What the hell we got to vote for?" Mickey says, completely out of the loop. When it comes to school busi-ness, Mickey couldn't care less. She might as well not even come to school sometimes, as oblivious as she is to the ins and outs of Drama High. All she cares about is what she's wearing, who's hating, and getting her diploma on time so she can go to beauty college. Everything else is secondary.

"Girl, where you been?" Nellie asks. "You have to vote for

the top three candidates for each grade level," she says, filling Mickey in while I retrieve my books from my locker. The bell has just rung and the race is on, with students bustling around the spacious hall, rushing off to first period.

"I don't get it. If you're nominated, doesn't that mean you've already been voted in?" Mickey asks, putting her man on hold to get a better understanding of the voting process. I guess she cares now that her girl's on the ballot. Jeremy shakes his head, amused by my girls' conversation.

"No, silly. I have to win a place on the actual ballot for next week's election. This is just the beginning," Nellie says all dreamy as if she's running for Miss America.

"Shit, that means I have to vote twice," Mickey says, resuming her phone conversation. "Baby, I got to go. The bell's about to ring," she says before hanging up her cell.

"That goes for me too," Jeremy says, giving me a kiss before sprinting down the hall. "Check y'all later," he says to my girls.

"Bye, Jeremy," they say at once.

"So, when is the voting supposed to take place?" Mickey asks, truly annoyed. Anything that takes away from her chill time aggravates her.

"At lunch. And the finalists will be announced Wednesday at break. Make sure you tell everybody in your classes, Jayd. I have to make it onto the ballot," Nellie says as we all head toward our respective classes.

"Will do, Princess," I say, teasing her. I'm sure she's popular enough to make the ballot on her own accord. I really don't want to get involved with all the election business. It's too volatile here. These folks take their politics very seriously, as Nellie will soon find out.

When I get to Spanish class I notice our teacher/football coach, Mr. Donald, is wearing a dress shirt and tie like he does on game day every Friday during the regular football season. I wonder what's going on.

"Good morning, class," Mr. Donald says, waiting for the bell to finish ringing before continuing. "I have a new student coming in this morning and I'll need to talk to him outside for a few minutes. You'll need to complete page eight in your workbooks. And, if you finish before we're done outside, you can start your homework on page twenty-five of your textbooks," he says, picking up his teacher's edition and writing the homework assignment on the board under today's notes.

When I reach into my backpack on the floor next to my seat, I notice my workbook's not in there. Damn it. I can't go more than two days without leaving one of my Spanish books in my locker. Reluctantly, I have to ask for yet another hall pass.

"Mr. Donald?" I ask while raising my hand. He doesn't need to turn from the board to look at me. He already knows what I'm going to say.

"Let me guess, Miss Jackson," he says. "You left your books in your locker."

"Yes, I did," I say. "I'm usually not this forgetful." Mr. Donald turns toward the class and looks straight at me with no emotion.

"Here, Miss Jackson," he says, handing me the hall pass. "And, please make this the last time."

"Thank you and I will," I say, feeling a little embarrassed. I like to remain somewhat anonymous in my elective courses. I just want to pass, not make friends or enemies.

As I rise from my desk to open the door, someone's already on the other side pushing it open. I step outside, almost losing my footing, to see a face from the past.

"There she is," Nigel, my old friend from back in the day, says as he releases the door to give me a tight hug. "How's my girl been?" he asks. He looks too good to be visiting, dressed in a dark blue pin-striped suit and hat to match.

"Nigel, what's up?" I say as he lets me go just enough to look up at him. Damn, he gives good hugs. "And more importantly, what are you doing here?"

"Girl, it's been a while and we miss you around the way," he says, allowing the door to completely close and leaving us outside to quickly catch up.

By his "we" I know he means Raheem. Whenever we'd get in a fight, which was often, Nigel would always play the middle man. But, this is the longest we've gone without talking, mostly due to us all leaving our old school, Family Christian, at the same time. Both of them now live in Windsor Hills, which isn't far from Inglewood, but is still a completely different hood from my mom's.

"A while? Try two years," I say, releasing myself from his embrace to look him in the eye.

"So, you're balling like that now, huh?" he says, grabbing my wrist and eyeing my gold bracelet. "Must be nice chilling with the White folks," he says. "But I'll know soon enough."

"What do you mean by that?" I ask, eyeing the hall clock. "Is Westingle turning all White or something?" I say, referring to their school. It's basically the Black South Bay High. My mom tried to get me to go there, but no such luck. Her address wasn't in the right area and she missed the deadline for submitting a transfer request.

"No, but the coaches from South Bay said they could promise me a starting position, basically guaranteeing me playing time in front of recruiters from the top colleges in the nation, which means scholarships. Now, a brotha can't pass that up, can I?" he says.

"So, you mean to tell me you're going to my school?" I ask, almost shouting. Oh, hell no. This can't be good. And, knowing Raheem, he'll be at every game, if not trying to transfer himself. They are each other's clique, no other members allowed or needed.

"Yeah, you got a problem with that?" Nigel asks, smiling.

"No, not at all," I say as Mr. Donald opens the door. But, hell yeah I got a problem with it. First Nellie's nomination, and now this. What the hell?

"Jayd, you know our new student, Nigel?" Yeah, a little too well. But, Mr. Donald doesn't need to know all that.

"Yeah, me and my girl here go way back," he says, putting his arm around me and giving me one last hug before I head to the Main Hall.

"I was just going to get my book," I say, leaving the two of them to talk.

"I'll catch up with you later, Jayd. Raheem gave me a letter for you, but I left it in my locker." A letter saying what, I wonder? All I need is more drama to deal with.

After voting, Nellie, Mickey and I decide to hang in South Central for the remainder of lunch. Although I miss my man, I need to chill with my friends too. Most of the usual suspects are still voting in the cafeteria. So, it's unusually peaceful in the quad area.

"Do you think I made it?" Nellie asks.

"I think so. The other names on the ballot weren't nearly as recognizable as yours. Well, except for Laura," I say. Laura's the first lady of ASB and that unofficial position always has its perks.

"What's the big deal?" Mickey says, picking at her hamburger. We each settled for cafeteria food today, which isn't so bad. But, the voting line was long and our food has gotten cold. "So what if you don't win. Does it really matter?" The look on Nellie's face surely makes Mickey regret her statement.

"How can you say that?" Nellie asks, beginning what I predict to be the tantrum of all tantrums. Whenever her voice raises ten octaves, I know she's about to throw a fit. "This is very important to me. And, it's good for our social status," she says, giving Mickey the evil eye.

"OK, whatever. Slow your roll and bring it down a notch," Mickey says, taking a bite out of her lukewarm burger. "All I meant was you shouldn't be disappointed if you don't win."

"That's just the type of negative thinking I don't need. And besides, I wouldn't be worried about our social status if Jayd had come to Byron's party with us as planned," Nellie says, bringing up old news.

"Why are you dragging me into this?" I say as I get up from the bench where we're seated to throw away my chili fries. If there's one thing I can't stand, it's cold potatoes.

"Because, Jayd, not showing up to Byron's party wasn't a good move. It seems like you just don't care about your popularity anymore," Nellie says, sounding truly concerned. "Yes, it helps that you're dating Jeremy. But, he's not concerned with popularity at all and that's OK for him. He's a rich White boy. You on the other hand, need to think more seriously about your reputation." Both Mickey and I look at Nellie like she's lost her damned mind.

"What the hell are you talking about?" Mickey says, finishing off the last of her fries. To be as skinny as she is, the girl can out eat me and Nellie combined.

"I'm talking about me winning. It doesn't help my campaign if I hang out with someone whose reputation is taking a turn for the worst."

"What the hell!" I exclaim, almost choking on my Coke. "My reputation is just fine, contrary to popular belief. And besides, if it weren't for your affiliation with me you wouldn't have been nominated in the first place," I say, checking my uppity friend. Just then, Misty, KJ, and Shae return from the cafeteria to their usual post at the table across from our bench.

"Hey, y'all," KJ says, smiling at me like he's just won something special.

"Hey, KJ," Nellie says. Mickey and I are still in a state of shock over Nellie's growing head.

"I don't even need to ask who y'all voted for, do I?" Nellie says, hot on her campaign trail. She's taking this princess thing a little too seriously. But, I guess Seth had it right this morning. Nellie does have just enough bitch in her to make it to the top.

"Of course we voted for you, Nellie. I made sure everyone in South Central did," KJ says, unwrapping his sub sandwich while Misty sits next to him, holding his Snapple in her hand. This girl's so sprung on him I'm almost embarrassed for her.

"Yeah. We Black folks stick together, ain't that right, Mickey?" Shae says, obviously trying to say something to me without directly saying it.

"Don't ask me. I couldn't care less about all this homecoming shit. Although I am going to the dance." Now, that's a shocker. Last year her man was on lockdown in county jail and Mickey didn't attend any school functions. But, this year is different, I guess.

"And, was that supposed to mean something to me, Shae?" I ask. I don't really want to confront her, but I can't let her get away with that little comment of hers. How come she thinks I'm such a sellout? Black folks get on my nerves with that mess.

"Not at all," Shae says, smiling. "I'm just saying if there's a Black name on the ballot, you know we're going to pick it because that's how we get down over here." Yeah, broad, clean it up why don't you. Frankly, I've had enough of her and Nellie. Besides, I can't stand to watch Misty practically feed KJ for another second. I wonder what my man is up to. Maybe I can catch up with him on my way to drama class.

"Well, as lovely as this little chat has been, I've got to roll," I say, grabbing my backpack from the ground before getting up to leave.

"Can't keep the White boy waiting, huh?" Misty says.

"Better than being someone's maidservant," I snap back at her before saying bye to my girls and heading away from the quad and down the hill. "I'll catch up with y'all after school," I say to Nellie and Mickey, ignoring Misty's evil glare and KJ's intense eyes.

"Jayd, I'll walk with you," Nellie says, hurriedly picking up her bag and tossing the rest of her chicken strips into the trash can before following me. It's not like her to leave Mickey, so this must be good. "I'll see y'all in class," she says to Mickey and everyone else, since they all have fifth period together.

"Jayd, I'm sorry if I hurt your feelings about the whole reputation thing," she says. "I just never imagined I could get nominated at this school for anything," she says, looping her arm into mine, forcing me to listen. Honestly, I don't want her to win if this is what's going to happen to her. She's already enough to deal with. Becoming princess will just make her ass even more uptight and stuck-up.

"I know. And, for the record, I couldn't care less about what people up here think of me," I say, not letting her completely off the hook while letting her know we're still cool.

"I know. And you're right. If it weren't for you, I wouldn't have been nominated. So, thank you, girl. This means so much to me," she says, returning to her princess dream. "I can't wait until the nominees are announced on Wednesday. I just know I'm going to win." For Nellie's sake, I hope if she does, that Matt, Seth, and Chance are going to be right there for her. Because, folks won't be happy with her nomination, and when the shit hits the fan, I don't know what she's going to do. She's never had to face any drama of her own up here. And, if my dream predicted correctly, there'll be plenty to go around.

~ 2 ~
Process of Elimination

"Walk like a champion,
Talk like a champion."

—BUJU BANTON

Although I'm a tad bit excited for Nellie, I honestly don't think today is going to be the grandiose picture she's painted for herself. She picked out a special outfit to wear for the big announcement and got her nails done after school yesterday. The girl's in the zone for winning the crown and nothing better get in her way. But, if I know one thing for sure, it's that something or someone's definitely going to try to spoil this coronation.

Speaking of which, these students around here seem to become ruder as the year progresses. What happened to a simple "excuse me" when you bump into someone? I've been standing in the Main Hall for five minutes where at least ten people have nudged my body in one way or another. And, according to my count, not a single one has said "excuse me". I turn around ready for the smackdown when one more person bumps into me.

"Oh. Excuse me, Jayd. My bad. I didn't see you standing there. *¿Que pasa, chica?*" Maggie says, giving me a big hug. At least someone else around here has some manners. "Why are you standing here by yourself? You know you and your girls should be rolling tight, with the announcement coming and all," she says referring to the impending backlash from the

White students and other haters, should Nellie win the nomination.

"I'm actually waiting for them. Mickey told me to meet them here at break and I haven't seen them yet," I say, getting a little worried. I hope the drama hasn't already begun. "How's your man?" I ask, surprised he's not with her. She and Juan are usually attached at the hip.

"Oh, he's fine. He's waiting for me in El Barrio. You want to hang with us while you wait?" Maggie asks, looping her arm into mine. "You know you're always welcome to hang with us, *hermana*," she smiles, reminding me why El Barrio is the tightest clique at South Bay. They even sound tight, always speaking in "we," like the Borg on *Star Trek: The Next Generation,* but definitely in a positive way.

"Maybe I should. Let me call Mickey and let her know where I'll be," I say, reaching for my cell with my free hand.

"By the way, how's your man?" Maggie asks. "I heard you and the White boy are pretty hot and heavy these days, no?"

My train of thought interrupted and briefly blushing, I proceed to scroll down my list of contacts until I reach Mickey's name and push send.

"He's just fine, and how did you know about the hot-and-heavy part?" I ask, ready to point the finger at Misty, the usual suspect. Mickey's voice mail picks up immediately, which means she's either on a call or turned off her phone. No point in leaving a message. I'm sure I'll see her before she gets around to checking her voice mail, one of her least favorite activities.

"Oh, don't you worry about that. We've got eyes and ears all over this campus. You just worry about pleasing your man. I like this Jeremy. He seems good for you, from what we've heard," she continues.

"What exactly have you heard and from where?" I ask.

"Well, not too much except he's very generous when it

comes to spoiling you," she says, gently touching the gold bangle Jeremy bought me last week. "And, that's a sure sign of a good man. Speaking of which, are you coming with us or not because Juan's about to send out the search party if I don't get my fine ass over there soon," she says, turning toward the quad area.

"You go ahead. I'd better stay here and wait for my girls," I say, still worried. Where are they?

"Suit yourself, chica. Tell Nellie and Mickey I said *hola* and your girl Nellie to watch her back. You know these people around here are serious about their crowns and shit," Maggie says, pulling her compact out of her backpack and checking her face in the tiny mirror.

"Will do, sis. I'll check for you later. We may need the backup if she wins," I say, only half joking. I'm expecting retaliation, but not immediately. These folks at South Bay High are stealthlike. Speaking of which, I see the ASB president headed this way. What's Reid up to now?

"Oh hell, here comes that corny White boy. Doesn't he have anything else better to do?" Maggie says as she returns her mirror to her backpack's side pocket and slips the huge Jansport onto her tiny back, ready to bolt. "*Adíos, chica. Hasta luego.*"

As Maggie heads down the crowded hall and out the double doors, I can't help but worry about my girls. Flipping my cell open to dial Nellie's number, even though I know her phone's usually off during school hours, Reid catches me off guard and hands me a flier for ASB's homecoming court nominees.

"Good morning, Miss Jackson. I haven't seen you at any of the meetings at lunch. It would really behoove you to stay affiliated with the right side," he says, leaning up against my locker.

"Reid, I'm always on the right side. Mine," I say, positioning myself away from him. "Why do you always talk to me like you're my daddy?"

Shifting his stocky frame from one side to the other, he smiles coyly while placing the stack of fliers he's holding directly in front of his chest so I can see the names. "Jayd, you used to be such a reasonable person. Do you honestly think Nellie's going to win today? If she does win a nomination, it's just a wasted spot that someone really worthy of wearing one of South Bay High's most prestigious crowns could hold, like our nominees."

"Don't you have some more fliers to pass out?" I say, not wanting to engage in a debate right now with this asshole. We were friendly opponents last year. But after the way he and his followers turned on me last year, I'm not feeling him anymore. Him helping me with my locker a couple of weeks ago doesn't change anything. He's one of the main reasons I don't associate with ASB anymore. They're the epitome of corrupt and he's definitely their leader.

"Yes, I do. But still, you should think seriously about what I've said. We need someone as outspoken as yourself on our team. Besides, it's always a good idea to surround yourself with winners. Not the losers you've recently selected to keep company with," he says looking past me. I turn to see what's caught Reid's attention.

Just in time, my girls, Jeremy, and Chance stroll up the hall in my direction. I turn back to Reid and look him square in the face.

"I hope you weren't referring to my girls, because those are fighting words." We used to spar often in ASB meetings and he always resorted to low blows, just like now. That's why we could never be real friends. At his core, Reid's a punk and I know it.

"No, not at all. I rather like Nellie and Mickey. They were at Byron's party, but you weren't, which was another bad move," he says, looking more serious than necessary. Reid's starting to give me the creeps.

"Hey, girl. Sorry we kept you waiting, but Miss Diva here had to change into her announcement outfit in the gym," Mickey says, making fun of Nellie, who's stunning in her simple black Chanel dress and matching heels.

"You are way too fancy for school, Miss Thang," I say, giving her a big hug. "But, you do look good. How are you going to outdress yourself for the dance?" I ask as I walk up to Jeremy and Chance standing behind Nellie and opposite Reid, our common enemy.

"Reid, what are you doing at my girl's locker?" Jeremy says in a very serious and almost threatening tone.

"Hello, ladies," Reid says, completely ignoring Jeremy. Just then, Jeremy steps in front of me and toward Reid, like he's ready to sock the snot out of him with Chance right by his side.

"Don't act like you didn't hear me, punk. I asked what you're doing here."

"Calm down, weiner boy," Reid says, purposely mispronouncing Jeremy's last name, which usually doesn't bother Jeremy since it's a common problem. But, I can see anything that comes out of Reid's mouth is enough to set Jeremy off. "We were just catching up on old times. Isn't that right, Jayd?" he says.

"Hell no. This fool's trying to push his little girlfriend Laura for junior class princess knowing my girl's running for the same spot," I say, making sure the lines of division are drawn clearly for Reid. I don't know what's up between him and Jeremy, but I'm damn sure not going to let him put me in the middle of it. Before I can say anything more, a voice comes across the loud speaker. The announcement is about to be made.

"This is your ASB coordinator, Ms. Toni, and I have two

very special announcements. One, of course, is the finalist for this year's homecoming princesses and queen." Everyone in the Main Hall and outside has stopped to listen. There's a buzz of excitement all around. "The way this works is simple," Ms. Toni continues. "There are three final candidates for each class. For the senior class, there are also three candidates. But, the seniors have two crowns available: one for the princess, who is the runner-up, and one for the queen."

"I really should be with the rest of ASB. Think about what I said, Jayd. Ladies." Reid gestures my girls a farewell nod and heads off, practically running away from Chance and Jeremy.

"Stay away from my folks, man. I'm not warning you again," Jeremy shouts after Reid, completely ignoring the people watching him in the unusually still corridor. I knew Jeremy didn't like the dude, but this feels like some deeper mess going on here. I'll have to pump him and Chance later for more information.

"The finalists are . . ." Nellie grabs mine and Mickey's hands. Jeremy and Chance stand right behind us.

"You're going to win girl. Just wait, it's yours," Chance says, looking down as Nellie smiles, thankful for his support.

"For freshman princess, the finalists are . . ." Other students are making drumroll sounds with their pencils and notebooks. "Candice Sheryl, Lucinda Bergen, and Cathy Rowe." Loud screams can be heard across campus, some happy, some sad. All accompanied by tears.

"Sophomore princess finalists are as follows: Julie Kendall, Mary Brillstein, and Becky Rainey."

"OK. Here it comes. Y'all pray for me," Nellie says, suddenly spiritual.

"The junior class nominees are," Ms. Toni continues, sounding as sassy as ever. "Katrina Carr, Laura Bland, and Nellie Smith."

"Aaah!" Nellie screams as she and Mickey embrace and

jump up and down, causing a huge scene. Misty and KJ are also in the hall, laughing at the sight.

"I knew you could do it," Chance says, picking Nellie up off the floor after Mickey lets her go. Nellie's so excited she doesn't even notice Chance sneak in a kiss on the cheek.

"Jayd, I made it on the ballot!" she screams in my face. I give my girl a big hug.

"Congratulations. You're on your way now, girl," I say, only slightly enthused. I'm too worried about the imminent backlash to get caught up in the hype of the moment.

"And, the senior class nominees for homecoming princess and queen are Kate Roberts, Josie Davis, and Tania Mahyari." Oh, hell no, Jeremy's ex isn't running for homecoming queen. I don't even think Nellie heard the list; she's so excited about her own name having been called. I look at Jeremy, whose reaction to Tania's name is nonexistent. But, he and Chance both notice my response.

"Problem, Jayd?" Chance asks as we shield ourselves from all of the excitement around us as people congratulate Nellie. Nellie is on cloud nine and Mickey's right up there with her for support.

"No, not at all," I say, insincerely. Of course there's a problem. How can Tania be nominated for homecoming court when she's barely here? And, I wonder if Jeremy knew she was running? Now I'll have to see her face everywhere, not just in third period. What the hell?

"There's one more special announcement I have to make," Ms. Toni says, silencing the loud hall. "We have a new quarterback coming to us from Westingle High School." I spoke to Nigel briefly on the phone yesterday after school. He was too busy being introduced to all of his teachers and teammates to give me the letter. It's been on my mind since yesterday morning. What could Raheem have to say to me after all this time? And, more importantly, do I tell Jeremy about it?

"Please welcome the latest addition to our winning Sharks team, Nigel Esop."

"Did you hear that, Jayd? We got a new Black dude up here. This day can't get any better," Nellie says, still high.

"How do you know he's Black?" Chance asks, like his territory is under attack.

"Nigel Esop. Do you know any White folks who would name their son that?" Mickey says, making us all chuckle. She's right. There are just some names that are definitely Black-owned.

"We need to catch up with Seth and Matt before third period," Jeremy says, giving me a hug. "I'll see you in class."

"OK, baby," I say, relieved they're leaving me and my girls alone for a moment. I need to fill them in on Nigel.

"And, congrats, Nellie," Chance says, stealing another hug from her before following Jeremy out of the hall.

"Thank you," Nellie says.

"OK, you two, listen up," I say, like we only have five minutes to live. "I know Nigel from way back," I say, leading them out of the hall and into the courtyard toward my government class. We only have a minute or two before the bell rings and I need to give them the 411.

"Damn, Jayd. How do you know so many folks?" Mickey asks. "And, they always happen to be dudes."

"Can you hook a sistah up?" Nellie asks, completely self-absorbed.

"Would you two shut up and listen?" I say, becoming impatient. "Nigel's my ex boyfriend Raheem's best friend and my homie from back in the day. Apparently Raheem wrote me a letter and gave it to Nigel to give to me," I say, stopping in front of my class.

"So, what's the big deal? I'm sure it's just a friendly note to say hi and he's happy y'all can reconnect," Nellie says.

"Yeah, maybe a little too happy. I need y'all to pump info from him and see what he knows about the contents of the letter. I know he won't give it to y'all because he doesn't know y'all like that. But, maybe you can see if Raheem is still feeling me."

"Why can't you just ask him yourself?" Mickey asks. She wants to know the entire story and I ain't about to give it up that easily.

"Look, I don't have time to get into all of that right now. And besides, I promised Jeremy we'd have lunch together. So I won't see Nigel today, I'm sure."

"Even though I don't know the whole story, I think you're smart for staying clear of any potential drama right now, especially after all that went down between you and KJ last week," Nellie says, reminding me of Jeremy and KJ's fight at the mall. All I need is another dude in my life to make Jeremy jealous. "But, I don't have time to play twenty questions," Nellie says, looking in her compact mirror, admiring her chocolate complexion. This girl is too much. "I have a crown to win."

"Fine, Miss Compton USA. Mickey, can you please pump Nigel for info?"

"Sure thing. Come on, Nellie. Let's get to class," Mickey says as the bell for third rings. Jeremy runs by them on his way to our class. Why does there have to be so much drama so early on in our relationship? I can't wait to get home and tell Mama about my day.

After Jeremy drops me off at the bus stop by Mama's house, I decide to take the long way home to think about my day. Between Nellie's nomination and Nigel's transfer, I can't concentrate on anything.

When I finally get home, Mama's in the kitchen cooking spaghetti, cabbage, and corn bread. The smell coming from the kitchen makes my stomach growl.

"Hey, baby. I thought I felt you walking up the street," Mama says. She's in her usual housedress, stirring the spaghetti sauce inside a big stainless-steel pot on the stove. The cabbage and corn bread are done and sitting on the kitchen table, waiting to be devoured. And, I'm up for the task.

"Hey, Mama," I say, giving her a kiss on the cheek before washing my hands in the sink and taking a seat at the kitchen table. Mama hasn't cooked in a week or so due to her busy schedule and the fact that she's supposed to be on strike from cooking for the men. But, there's enough food here to feed an army. And, when my uncles and grandfather come home, it'll be time for the war.

"How was your day?" she says, taking the large wooden spoon out of the pot and putting it into the full sink.

"It was very exciting," I say, recalling the day's events in my head.

"Really? Exciting good or exciting bad?" she says, studying my face. I can never get anything past Mama.

"Well, I don't know yet," I say. "Nellie won the nomination for homecoming princess."

"Well, that's good news, isn't it?" she asks. I'm not really sure how to answer that question without getting into the details of Monday's dream. Knowing Mama, she'll make me analyze it, write it down, and then assign homework based on it. And, I'm not in the mood for more work right now. But, I could use some advice about Nigel.

"Yes, it's great for her. And, Nigel is the newest member of South Bay's elite Black population," I add, taking a nibble from the corn bread. It's still in the cast-iron skillet and steaming, just the way I like it.

"Nigel from Family Christian Nigel?" she asks, turning off the pot of spaghetti before sitting down across from me. Lexi, Mama's canine shadow, is under the table, fast asleep.

"Yes, the very same one. But, he and Raheem transferred to Westingle last I heard and Raheem sent a letter for me through him."

"Well, if Nigel's on the prowl, you know Raheem ain't far behind. When's the last time you talked to that boy?" Mama says with a little disgust in her voice. All Mama remembers about Raheem is the bad stuff. Like us getting caught kissing behind the bleachers in the seventh grade, making out in the girl's restroom in the eighth and him getting my best friend at the time pregnant in the ninth. Hard to believe I was actually in love with him.

"Not since I chewed him out for kissing Nia," I say, referring to his illicit affair with my cousin on my dad's side our last year at Family Christian. The boy gets around.

"Damn, Jayd. I hoped you would escape the constant man problems of the William's women legacy. Or at least that part of it," Mama says nibbling on the still hot corn bread with me. Nobody makes buttermilk corn bread like Mama can.

"What legacy?" I ask, anxious for a good story. There's always a lesson involved. Before she answers, I get up and make a plate and pour myself a large glass of Tropical Punch Kool Aid with lemons. After I've gotten my food, I settle in my seat. It's only the two of us here now. So, it's a good time to have a little girl chat.

"The lesson of heartbreak from choosing the wrong men," she says, cutting a slice of corn bread and placing it on my overstuffed plate. This is one of my favorite meals. Mama doesn't eat until everything's cooled off. For some reason, she doesn't like her food hot, unlike me. I prefer it fresh off the stove, damn near burning my tongue, when possible.

"How's Jeremy?" she asks, making me smile. In spite of all the day's drama, the highlight was a quiet lunch with Jeremy at the beach and a slow ride home. I just love the way he makes me feel. And, I love that he loves being with me too.

"He's good. We're good. That's why I'm afraid of Nigel coming in and interrupting our flow," I say, stuffing a forkful of spaghetti into my mouth. This is the best comfort food ever.

"He can't interrupt anything unless you let him, Jayd. Don't you get that by now?" she asks. "You, as the female, have all the power in relationships." Huh? Mama must be talking about some other kind of relationship because all the relationships I've seen, usually the men are the ones in power.

"Mama, are you serious?" I ask.

"Very," she says, getting up and walking over to the refrigerator. She reaches up to the top and takes down her secret recipe book, which is where she keeps it when it's not in her spirit room.

"Here's the story of my mother, Marie, and my father, Jon Paul Williams," she says, turning to a chapter I've never seen before. This book is so huge it would take me years to read through cover to cover. There are fifteen sections, all meticulously divided and color-coded for easy reference. So far I've only ventured to the recipes section for my personal use.

The last time I was at the beauty shop with Mama, Netta mentioned Mama's parents, but we didn't get into it. All I know is Mama's mother was a white woman from Paris and her father a dark Haitian man. Mama doesn't talk much about her parents because she didn't grow up with them. But, the little I do know is that Mama believes her father drowned her mother in the bathtub because of jealousy. Now, that's some shit to live with.

"Jayd, men are powerful beings, physically. But, spiritually, women are where it's at," she says, flipping through the yellowed pages before stopping at a page with a picture of a woman on it.

"Is this your mother?" I ask, taking a large gulp of my Kool Aid.

"Yes. This is your great-grandmother, Maman Marie Devereaux." Mama stares at the sketch hard, like she's communicating with her mother's spirit. "Contrary to popular belief, my mother wasn't a White woman, although she could easily pass for one. Her mother was white and her father was a light-skinned Black man, like your daddy." Maybe that's why she hates my father so much.

"So, why didn't you correct Netta when she was telling your story?" I ask, referring to Netta's infatuation with Mama's lineage.

"Because it ain't her story to tell in the first place," Mama says, snappily. "People love to talk, Jayd, especially if the story being told is so juicy it sounds more like a legend than real life. And most of the time, the people talking only know part of the story." As Mama continues, I clear the table of my empty dishes. But I'm anxious to settle back into my seat and see where Mama's going with this.

"Maman was born in California. She moved to Paris in the late 1940s when she was a teenager to study art, I guess. I don't know the full story. But, I've written down everything I heard about her as the years passed," she says, staring at her mother's picture. The woman in the photograph is very light with straight, black hair. Even though it's a black-and-white photograph, I can still see her fierce green eyes, just like Mama's and my mother's.

"Part of your legacy is power. And people—men especially—are attracted to power. Maman was the most powerful of us all," Mama says, a little teary-eyed. "I didn't get a chance to know my mother, being that she died before my first birthday, and then I was sent to live with my daddy's relatives in New Orleans after he disappeared. Dirty bastard. But, I still know her spirit," she says, taking a paper towel from the roll on the table and wiping her eyes.

"What was her power?" I ask, knowing each of the Williams women have special gifts. Mama's ability is to heal and see things as they happen, before they happen, and after they happen. My ability is to dream and sometimes I get premonitions. I'm not sure about my mother and auntie because they never developed their powers, according to Mama.

"Is, Jayd. Is. All of the ancestors on my shrine are still alive because I call on them and remember them," she says. "That is also the power of your legacy. You can call on your ancestors anytime you need to and they will be right there. But, be careful who you call on. Not all ancestors are good," she says, sending a chill up my spine.

"OK, what is Maman's power?" I ask, a little shaken by Mama's tone.

"She has the power to help those in need, to heal, and to change the future, which is why my father killed her," she says point blank. "He was jealous because she possessed the power he so craved," she says, turning the pages. "Jon Paul's family—the Williams—are from Haiti, and yes, he was a Vodoun priest. But, not the good kind. He was greedy and wanted to use his power for selfish motivations. Not to help people, like Maman." Lexi shuffles under the table.

"I'm telling you all this to say be careful, Jayd. Men do some strange things to get what they want. And, you obviously have something these boys desire. Even without the full gift of sight, your pull is strong. It's no coincidence Nigel's at South Bay. You better find out what Raheem wants with you before you make a huge mistake and sacrifice your relationship with Jeremy," she says, taking out her writing tablet from the back of the book and writing down my assignment, I assume. Mama's on point with that one. I want to know what Raheem wants too.

"Read Maman's story and write down as many points as you can make out of it. We'll talk about it when you're done. Right now I have to get this food down to Mrs. Webb," she says, referring to our neighbor at the end of the block. She just lost one of her sons in a car accident.

"So, this food isn't for the house?" I ask, sorry to see all the good food leave.

"Hell no. I'm through cooking for these fools," she says, rising from the table. "But, you can make your cousin Jay a plate. He should be home any minute now," she says, looking up at the wall clock. It's almost eight and I need to get started on my homework. I also need to talk to Nigel about Raheem's letter. But, knowing him, he's still at football practice.

As I get up from my comfortable seat to make Jay's plate, Mama's words are heavy on my heart. What do these dudes want with me? Well, I guess I'll have to wait and see. But, she's right. I need to stop this storm before it starts.

~ 3 ~
Damage Control

"Outcasts and girls with ambition/
That's what I wanna see."

—PINK

It's Friday and the homecoming buzz is all around. It's only been two days since the finalists were announced and there are already posters of the candidates all over campus. I feel for Nellie being one of the Drama Club's candidates. Not because we're not organized, but because we aren't all that visible on campus unless we're on stage. We're good at performing and talking shit. But, when it comes to making signs, posters, and all the campaign tools necessary to win, that just ain't our thang.

And, as if there wasn't enough tension in my life, Jeremy springs on me this morning that he doesn't do dances. Some bullshit about him and his brothers making a pact years back. It's been on my mind since we pulled up to campus and I can't wait to catch up with him again today so we can finish our discussion. What the hell?

"Hey, Jayd," Nigel calls down the hall after me. "Wait up." It's break and I want to catch up with my girls and Jeremy. But, I'm glad to see Nigel too. I want my letter.

"You must be the busiest Black man at South Bay High," I say, giving him a hug. The other students in the Main Hall notice us and I feel self-conscious. I don't want Jeremy or Misty to get wind of me being too friendly with the new guy. "Where's my letter?" I ask.

"A little anxious, are we?" Nigel teases. It feels just like old times. "I met your girls, secret agent double-o-seven," he says, taking what I assume to be my letter out of his backpack. "What kinda friend you think I am? You knew I wasn't going to tell them girls nothing," he says, waving the letter in my face.

"Well, if you would have simply come back to Mr. Donald's class the same day and given me the letter, I wouldn't have to send my girls on a mission," I say as I reach for the letter. "Would you please give it to me?"

"I knew you wanted me, Jayd, but damn. You don't have to beg," he says, laughing at his own joke.

"You're so stupid, Nigel. Give me the damned letter," I yell, tired of his behavior. Why do boys have to play so much?

"All you have to do is say please," he says, handing me the letter I've waited all week to read. It had better be good.

"I got to meet up with coach before class," Nigel says. He's always been a dedicated athlete and student, as well as a serious rapper. Gotta love a well-rounded brother. And, many sisters do. "I sent a little message for you through your girls. Holla," he says before sprinting down the hall. Now I can read my letter in peace.

I walk outside class since it doesn't look like I'm going to catch up with anyone before the bell rings in the next minute. Leaning up against a tree outside Government class, I open the sealed envelop with the letter *J* on it and unfold the paper inside.

> Jayd, I miss you. Call me.
> Same number, same Rah.
> Peace.

That's it? That's so typical of Rah to leave me hanging. He's always been a man of a few words, unlike KJ and very much like Jeremy. I want to talk to Nigel more, but I'm trying to keep my association with him on the low for as long as possible. I'll have to see what Mickey came up with at lunch.

As we make ourselves comfortable on a bench outside the library, Nellie, Mickey, and I begin to dish on Nigel. No one is likely to hear us here.

"So, Miss America, how's the campaign going?" Mickey says, making me wait for my news.

"It's a little slow. What I really need is a campaign manager who's known by everybody and respected by most. The Drama Club gets no love among the majority of the other cliques and I don't really like talking to people, which makes it damn near impossible for me to reach my constituents," Nellie says, flipping her hair over her shoulders and then studying her French manicure. She's such a princess, and most of the time, I love her for it.

"Your constituents," Mickey asks incredulously.

"Yes. My constituents. The people need a real campaign. Like that girl Laura. Her face is plastered all over the place. I can't even squat in the girl's restroom without seeing her campaign posters. What makes her so hot?" she asks, dipping her celery sticks into a plastic container full of ranch dressing before taking a bite. We all decided to be good today and have salads from the cafeteria.

"Nellie, Laura's boyfriend is the Associated Student Body president. Of course her campaign's going to be more visible," I offer, not sure I'm really helping. But, it's the truth. It'll take a miracle for Nellie to win this race. "Besides, the Drama Club has it's own campaign strategy, to pull the votes in during our killer performance homecoming week. I'm sure your campaign will be just fine."

"Maybe you should be her campaign manager," Mickey says, only half serious, I hope.

"Oh, hell no," I say, cutting off Nellie's response.

"But, why not? You're the natural choice, Jayd. You're in the Drama Club, you're my friend, and you used to be in ASB, so you know what we're up against," Nellie reasons. But I'm not budging.

"I have enough drama of my own, thank you very much, which moves us to the next item on our agenda. What did you get out of Nigel?" I ask, almost whispering in between bites of my oversize salad. It's like the salad bar at Sizzler's in our cafeteria.

"Yeah. Is he taken? Because if not, you can slip him my number. It would be so cute if we ended up at the dance together. He, the first Black quarterback and me, the first Black homecoming princess. Our names even sound good together: Nellie and Nigel, or Nigel and Nellie," she says, almost dreamlike.

"Well, he must be with someone because a brotha didn't even try and holla at all this," Mickey says, eyeing her reflection in the library door window.

"Hello? Back to me," I declare, reaching for my bottled water on the ground next to my backpack. It's October and still hot as hell out here by lunchtime.

"Oh yeah. He says you're missed," Mickey says, almost annoyed. "And to come to the studio tonight, if you're free, that is."

"The studio? Oh, no, not another wannabe rapper. Now I'm completely turned off," Nellie says, looking totally disgusted. "Why can't brothers just be football players or whatever their real talent is? Why everybody got to try to be a rapper?" she asks, finishing the last of her salad before opening her Snapple.

"Actually, rapping is his talent. Football's his hustle," I say, checking Nellie's snobbish attitude. I remember the first time Raheem took me to his homemade studio in his mother's garage. When I heard his beats and Nigel's rhymes I knew they would make it big one day soon.

"Oh, yeah? And, what's Raheem's talent?" she retorts, making me a little flustered.

"His talent is producing and mixing sounds. They're actually a really good team," I say as I get up to throw the remainder of my salad in the trash can.

"And, does Raheem also have a hustle?" Mickey asks with a devilish smile.

"Yes, he does. But, that's none of your business," I say, not wanting to give up too much information on my boy. "Raheem's actually a very intelligent brotha. He's planning on studying law and becoming an entertainment lawyer, as well as a producer."

"And you sound like his first groupie," Nellie says.

"Actually, that's a story for another day," I say, remembering my first kiss with Raheem. It tasted like chocolate milk and Doritos. It was my first kiss and his too. We were each other's first everything. Well, almost everything.

"Ooh, sounds like this is going to be good," Mickey says, ready for the scoop. But, I'm holding out on full disclosure for as long as possible.

"I ain't telling y'all nosy heffas nothing," I say.

"Come on, Jayd. We won't tell your dirty little secrets. What did y'all do?" Mickey asks.

"None of your business," I say, a little flushed. She's bringing up memories of me and Rah making out when I had full sensation in my breasts before my reduction.

"So, are you going to the studio? He says the session's tomorrow night and you know the spot and time," Mickey says, not letting it go.

"I don't know. I don't think Jeremy would be too happy with me going to my ex's for a late-night rhyme session," I say, missing my man.

"That's right, Jayd. You and Jeremy just started life as a couple a few days ago. Don't go ruining it over some wannabe Tupac," Nellie agrees, picking up her and Mickey's trash and taking it to the trash can.

"Don't listen to her, Jayd. Nigel seemed to genuinely miss you and says Raheem does too. I think you should at least reach out," Mickey says, handing me a piece of paper with both Nigel and Raheem's cell numbers on it. "Did you get the letter?" she asks.

"Yeah, but it didn't say much," I say, taking the envelope out of my backpack and handing it to Mickey.

"Jayd, you don't need no more drama, especially if you're going to be my campaign manager," Nellie says as she sits down next to me, reaching for the paper with their numbers on it and ignoring my first rejection.

"Nellie, I'm not heading your campaign for the slaughter house," I say, instantly feeling bad for doubting my friend's chances at winning. But, the dream I had the other night is still haunting me. Should I tell her about it? Will she see it as a warning or me being a typical jealous female? Either way, I'm keeping my mouth shut on all fronts.

"It won't be a slaughter if you manage my public persona," Nellie says, sounding sincere. Shit. Why is she dragging me into this?

"Come on, Jayd. You're good at this kind of stuff, and you know damn near everybody of influence up here," Mickey says, getting up from her spot at the other end of the bench to stretch her long, thin legs. She could easily be America's Next Top Model.

"Please? I'll be extra nice to your boyfriend, whoever he turns out to be," Nellie says, giving me a hug with her silly ass to seal the deal. Even though I really don't want to manage her homecoming campaign, I'd feel bad if I didn't. I've got to help my girl out or she'll be butchered by the competition.

"You know you owe me for this," I say.

"Aah, thank you, Jayd. I'll never forget this," Nellie says, hugging me so hard we almost fall of the bench.

"OK, now that we've got that out the way, what are you going to do about Nigel?" Mickey asks.

"Well, I'm going to my mom's house tonight anyway. Maybe I'll go just for a little while."

"Don't worry, girl. We got your back," Mickey says. "If Jeremy asks what you're doing tonight, just tell him you're hanging out with us," she says, immediately looking at Nellie for her anticipated disapproval of lying.

"What? Why y'all looking at me?" she asks.

"You don't have a problem with providing Jayd with a false alibi?" Mickey challenges Nellie.

"Not at all. I told you, Jayd: I owe you for this. Now, let's talk about our platform," Nellie says, reaching into my backpack to retrieve a pen and writing paper.

"You better use these couple of weeks to your advantage, Jayd. You may not ever get her to be this flexible again," Mickey says just as the bell signaling the end of lunch rings. I missed spending it with Jeremy. But, since he's taking me to my mom's tonight, I wanted to spend this time with my girls instead.

"If I win," Nellie says, putting the pen and paper back into my backpack and leading the way toward the Main Hall, "you'll never have to hear a word of disapproval about any of the poor decisions you make in the men you date ever again."

"Was that supposed to be a kind remark?" I ask, not quite sure if I should be insulted or not.

"Yes, of course it was. And, what's so special about Nigel and Raheem anyway?" she asks, obviously not knowing about the brothas at Westingle High.

"Well, you tell me, Mrs. N & N, or did you forget the monograms you already have engraved in your pretty little head?" I say, reminding her a few minutes ago she was sprung on Nigel her damned self.

"Yes, but I was just joking and judging him from his public persona here. But, to lie to your man? Now, I don't know if he's that special."

"He's not, but Raheem is, huh, Jayd?" Mickey asks, barely missing running into the people rushing past us as we slowly make our way to class.

"Mickey, it's not like that. I'm going to tell Jeremy exactly where I'm going if he asks."

"OK, but back to my original question. What's so special about them?" Nellie says.

"Where do I begin," I say, reminiscing about my days as Raheem's woman. "Being with cats from Westingle is a whole other experience," I say as we continue our walk toward the Main Hall. Granted, I wasn't with Raheem when he started his new school. But, he and Nigel fit right in with those brothers, I'm sure. I know plenty of them from working at Simply Wholesome. They are all fine and intelligent, just like Rah and Nigel. "The brothas at Westingle are all cocky, but not like KJ: They actually have all the right shit to be cocky about."

"Shit like what?" Nellie asks, leading the way down the long corridor toward our lockers. The hall is full of students rushing past us. I was supposed to meet up with Jeremy before going to fifth period, but I guess I'll have to wait to see him after school. This conversation's too important to leave hanging.

"Everything, y'all. The brothers are fine, clean cut, athletic, smart, wealthy, and they got street hustle, unlike KJ and his boys who just front. They also have no need to play games because they're wanted by every girl in sight," I say, feeling a twinge of pain as I remember the reason Raheem and I could never get it together.

"So, if they're so damn hot, then why aren't you still with your man?" Nellie asks, turning the twinge into a pang.

"Because they're too hot for my own good. Raheem wanted to have his fun and me too," I say as we approach Nellie's locker. Luckily, I don't need to bring books to my last two classes of the day, drama and dance. "Besides, we're much better off as friends, even though we haven't spoken in over a year."

"Hey, baby. I missed you at lunch today," Jeremy says, sneaking up behind me and giving me a great big bear hug. I love the way he feels.

"Hey, you," I say giving my girls the evil eye and turning around to kiss him. Why didn't they tell me he was coming?

"We'll call you later, Jayd. Bye, Jeremy," Mickey says as she leads Nellie down the hall toward their fifth period class.

"Bye, y'all," I say with hella attitude. "So, how was lunch with your boys?" I ask Jeremy as he takes my backpack in one hand and puts his other arm around my shoulders. I love when he walks me to class.

"It was cool. We just played hacky sack by the parking lot and shot the shit. Nothing special. How about you and your girls? Are they still giving you shit for being with me?" he says, smiling down at me with those pretty eyes.

"Not really. Nellie wants me to be her campaign manger and for you to take me to the dance," I say, hoping a little pressure from my girls will help change his mind. They actually don't know yet. But, I already know what they'll say.

"Well, you can get involved in the whole homecoming thing by being Nellie's campaign manager and going to the dance, but I'm sure they understand a man has his principles," he says, not bending at all.

"No, they don't, and frankly, neither do I."

"Can we talk about this later? I'm still taking you to Inglewood this afternoon, right?" he asks, reaching down to kiss me before beating the bell to his class.

"Yes, but this doesn't mean you're forgiven," I say, allowing him to kiss my pouty lips. His kisses are so tempting, but this dance is important to me and Nellie. He should come to offer his support if nothing else. "What's the big deal if you really don't care? Can't you just do it because it means a lot to me?" I ask, knowing he can't answer me right now.

"After school, Jayd. And, it's personal to me, baby. Real personal. I'll explain later." As I watch my man run down the hall, I wonder what I've really gotten myself into with this cat.

I'm glad the week is over. It's been hectic, trying to deal with Nellie's growing head and keeping my own cat from jumping out of the bag. I wonder how long I can keep my friendship with Nigel a secret from Jeremy. Not for long, if Misty has anything to say about it, I'm sure. I just hope my friendships with Nigel and Raheem don't ruin my relationship with Jeremy. Guys are so territorial when it comes to male friends. But, what's up with Jeremy not taking me to the first dance of the year? He better have a damn good excuse for this one.

As I walk up the hill from dance class and toward the Main Hall, I notice Misty and KJ walking toward the main parking lot. Where the hell are they going together? I know KJ ain't stupid enough to actually get with this girl.

"Hey, Jayd," KJ says as I walk past, trying not to look directly at them.

"Hey, KJ," I say, ignoring Misty. I should have known better than to trust her around KJ in the first place. Like Mama says, keep your friends close and your enemies closer. I momentarily let Misty out of my sight and she single-handedly ruins my relationship with KJ, gets me into some bullshit with his side trick Trecee, and now she's kicking it with him. Damn, she's good.

"Is KJ the only person you see?" Misty says. "I know you got better manners than that, Jayd." I stop dead in my tracks and look her straight in the eye. If I could blow her up I would.

"I don't speak to broads," I say, resuming my pace. I hope I can catch up with my girls before they head out. I knew Jeremy was going to take me to my Mom's house today, so I brought my weekend stuff to school and stuffed it into my locker.

When I reach my locker, Jeremy and my girls are already there waiting for me.

"Hey, Jayd. What took you so long? You almost missed us," Nellie says.

"Hey, baby," I say, stretching up to kiss my man and ignoring Nellie's impatience.

"Oh, OK. It's like that," Nellie says, playfully pushing me, knocking Jeremy and me off balance.

"Leave them alone," Mickey says, folding her cell shut. "You're just hating cause you ain't gotta man."

"That's not true," Nellie says, looking slightly embarrassed. "Don't you think I could have a man if I wanted one?"

"With your finicky, high-maintenance ass? Not really," Mickey says, further aggravating Nellie.

"I know someone who's interested," Jeremy says, of course referring to Chance. If the two of them got together, it would be a first for them both. Chance usually dates skanky White girls. And Nellie only dates Black dudes with hella Benjamins, which is why she's perpetually single.

"If you're talking about Chance, I'm cool. But, I am grateful to him for nominating me, which reminds me . . . Jayd, when are you going to get started on my campaign? I need posters, fliers, and buttons. I want the works. I want to give Laura what's-her-face a run for her money," she says, getting all riled up.

Students and faculty alike are clearing the halls, ready to leave South Bay High behind for the weekend. And frankly, so am I, even though I am kind of excited about helping my girl win. We need to break some new boundaries around this camp, regardless of what my dream predicts.

"Calm down, Nellie. I'll get started next week," I say retrieving my books and bag from my locker before slamming it shut. It's still a little sticky from the new paint. But, at least now I can get it open without any help. Jeremy instinctively grabs my backpack, leaving me to carry only my Gap Hobo bag full of my weekend stuff.

"Jayd, I want to win. So, don't sleep on it, OK? Come on, Mickey. I need to get to the mall to pick out my dress."

"Who the hell you do you think you are?" Mickey says. "I ain't your damn chauffeur."

"I didn't mean it like that," Nellie says, trying to clean up her mess. She knows better than to come at Mickey wrong. "I just meant I know you have to get home and I don't want to keep you."

"Yeah, whatever. I hope your ass don't win. You're already too much of a damn princess. See y'all later," Mickey says, giving me a hug. "And, have nice weekend, Jayd," she says, slyly referring to the session tonight with Raheem and Nigel.

"OK, Jayd. But, please get to work on my campaign strategies this weekend. Remember, it's for a good cause," Nellie says as she gives me a hug and Jeremy a pat on the shoulder. "Get my girl home safely. And, tell Chance if he gets a new car, I'll think about allowing him to take me to dinner."

"I'll give him the message," Jeremy says, laughing at my silly friend. As they head out of the Main Hall, Jeremy and I walk slowly in the same direction.

"That Nellie is something else," Jeremy says.

"Something else and much, much more." As we walk down the hill toward the back parking lot where Jeremy's parked, I notice the dark blue ocean water in the distance. I see boats dotting the horizon and surfers lost in the waves.

"Do you miss going to the beach with your friends after school?"

"Not when I'm hangin with you," he says, letting go of my hand and pulling me close to him.

"Well, if you like me so much, then why won't you take me to the dance?" I ask, ready to start the conversation he put on hold earlier.

"Like I said, it's personal, baby. And, it has nothing to do with my feelings for you."

"Well, then what is it? 'Cause, I don't understand. You see how excited Nellie is to be nominated. It means so much to her and to Chance. Can't you come to support our friends?" I ask, looking up at him poutily as we approach the car. Breaking our embrace, he opens the car door and tosses my backpack into the backseat before letting me in. When he takes his seat and starts the engine, he looks at me very seriously.

"Jayd, there's a lot of history between Reid's family and mine. And, because of my loyalty to my brothers, I don't support any function Reid has anything to do with. Dances and all." Being that part of ASB's duties is to put together all school dances, I guess he won't be taking me to a single one.

"But Jeremy, what about your loyalty to me? And, don't you want to see me in a sexy evening gown?" I ask, touching his thigh as we head out of the near empty parking lot toward Inglewood.

"Baby, like I said. It's personal. I hope you can understand I don't mean to hurt you. And, of course I want to see you all dressed up, as fine as you are. I tell you what. I'll come over and help you get dressed and I'll even take you and pick you up," he says, attempting a compromise. I know he's trying to be sweet, but all I can see is his stubbornness.

"Baby, please don't make me go alone," I say, almost pleading. I can just hear Misty, KJ, Shae, and the rest of South Central talking shit all night long if I come without my man. I'll never live it down.

"I'm not making you do anything. And, you won't be alone. There'll be plenty of people there, just not me. Besides, Jayd, dances are so boring to me. I'm just not into school functions like that." Well, I guess that's the end of that. Whatever happened between his and Reid's families must be pretty bad and I'm just dying to know what it is. But, I know better than to push him right now. I'll wait for a more suitable time, like when I'm nibbling his ear.

As we speed down Pacific Coast Highway, our conversation is quickly replaced by the radio. Listening to Gwen Stefani, I realize I ain't no hollaback girl, either. I'm going to the session tonight. I'll call Nigel as soon as I get to my Mom's house and let him know I'm coming. Besides, it'll be nice to see Raheem.

~ 4 ~
The Brothas at Westingle

*"You got what it takes to make me leave my man/
I just can't control myself."*

—LL COOL J/JENNIFER LOPEZ

After Jeremy drops me off, I bolt inside, call Nigel to let him know I need a ride, take a shower, press my hair, and put it in five cornrows with cowry shells at the end. It's the quickest I've ever done my hair. But, I don't want to hold Nigel up when he gets here. He said he'd be here at nine on the dot. Brothers may be late for school or a date. But, when it comes to sessions, they're always on time.

My mom's already out for the evening. According to the note she left on the fridge, she went to happy hour with her coworkers. I'm glad too because I needed to raid her closet to look my finest tonight. If I'm going to see Raheem I want to be as fly as possible. And, the clothes I left here last weekend are a little too casual for the studio. I settled on her black Baby Phat strapless gaucho jumpsuit and my black sandals. I know they both won't be able to take their eyes off of me tonight.

Luckily, Jeremy needed to get some studying done tonight. He also has to start filling out his college applications. I told him I was going to catch up on my beauty rest after doing my hair. I feel bad leaving out my little trip to Raheem's. But, some things are best kept secret, ya feel me?

* * *

When Nigel's green '64 Impala pulls up in front of my mom's apartment building, I remember why I like hanging with the brothas from Westingle. He and all of his homies are ballers in one way or another. They're also very intelligent and athletic, and all on their way to a UC or one of the private universities around here.

The Westingle brothas also come with their own kind of groupie broads. Also ballers and smarties, but broads just the same. Most of these girls are the ones Nellie wishes she were friends with. They shop only at the Beverly Center or on Melrose, buy top-of-the-line everything, and can afford to change Louis bags like Kimora Lee Simmons. I hope none of these broads are at the studio tonight. I'm just not in the mood for the hating.

"Hey, girl. Sorry to keep you waiting," Nigel says through the window. "The two La Breas always confuse me, especially at night. You know this ain't my territory," Nigel says, making it sound like he lives far. As he reaches across the passenger's seat to open the door, I begin to feel a little guilty. Should I go even though I neglected to inform Jeremy of my plans?

"You only live fifteen minutes up La Brea, fool," I say, taking my time getting in the car. People from Windsor Hills act like Inglewood doesn't exist.

"Well, are you getting in or not? You know session starts promptly at ten, baby girl. Don't worry, your White boy won't find us."

"Shut up, Nigel and don't rush me," I say, clutching the heavy metal door handle and sliding into the front seat. The matching green leather interior is clean and smooth, just like in Jeremy's car.

"I'm glad you decided to hang out with your old crew, Miss Lyttle," Nigel says, taking me back to my BGirl days while giving me a big hug. "For a minute I thought you were trying to hide from a nigga at that White ass school," he says, turning his radio down. "But, then your girl Mickey told me about your new man and I didn't want to cause you no trouble and shit. But, damn, Jayd. A White boy? I never pegged you for the type."

"I know. But, he's hella cool. I'll introduce y'all next week."

"That's alright. I've heard enough about him. It's you I'm concerned with," he says, looking at my hair and gear. "You're looking good, girl. Raheem's definitely going to be glad to see you," he says while pulling away from the curb toward Windsor Hills.

"So, you called him and told him you located Red October," I say, trying not to reveal my nervousness. Raheem has always had this affect on me. I remember the first time I saw him at our old school, Family Christian. He was in the eighth grade. I was in the seventh. It was puppy love at first sight. We went together for over two years. Well, he turned into a full grown dog a couple of years later, which is how we ended up where we are now: in unfamiliar territory.

"Hey, it wasn't like that," Nigel says, reaching over me and into the glove compartment to retrieve his CD case. "Your boy knew you'd been there for a year already and just wanted me to check you out, since we're schoolmates and all."

"And, why are we schoolmates?" I ask, wanting to know the real reason he transferred to South Bay High.

"Honestly, it's closer to my mom's house. And, I wanted to be near her," he says, sounding like a good son. He and his mother are very close. Like me, he's an only child. "At first it was cool going to Westingle. You know, the girls up there are hella fly," he says, taking a CD out of the case and popping it in the stereo. Smokey Robinson. The boy's got good taste. "But, gas is way too expensive to be rolling from Long Beach to Westchester every day."

"I know that's right," I say, agreeing the gas prices are out of control. But, as Daddy says, that's what happens when a Republican gets into office.

"So, South Bay High was the next best choice, because of their academics, and of course, the football program is top notch."

"Well, I'm glad to have another brotha in the mix," I say. It'll give the wannabe brothas up there, like KJ and his crew, someone to compete with. Then maybe we sistahs can benefit. Men are at their best when there's a little competition. As we cruise down La Brea toward Fairview Boulevard, I can't help but feel excited as we approach Raheem's house.

"So, how do you like South Bay High so far?" I ask, knowing it's a completely different world from Westingle. In Westchester, White folks are the minority. It's located between LAX and the Marina: prime real estate location for Los Angeles. And, wealthy Black and Asian kids are the majority and they're hella smart. Too bad my mom missed the deadline for me to transfer there. I'd probably have an entirely different story to tell, but with the same type of drama, I'm sure.

"The weather's the same. You know being by the beach is great for working out on the football field. But, the people are on some straight up Oreo shit, Jayd. Them brothers don't even act like real niggas up there. I can see why you got with a White dude," Nigel says, making me miss my baby. "So, I heard you went with the basketball star, KJ, too. You working it up there, huh, girl?" he asks, nudging my left knee with his right.

"Stop being nasty and keep your eyes on the road." As he makes the right onto Fairview, my stomach's getting all knotted up. I can't stand it. I'm too excited to see this boy. The last time I saw Raheem was over a year ago, before my breast reduction. He'd hurt me so bad I didn't ever want to have another boyfriend again in life. I wonder what he'll think of my new, much smaller appearance. He was the first boy to ever see my breasts under my shirt, so I'm sure he'll notice the difference, unlike Nigel. He probably thinks I just lost weight, like most people.

When we get to Raheem's house, his little brother, Kamal, is hangin' outside on the front porch listening to his iPod. Raheem's in the doorway behind him, talking on his Blackberry. I see not much has changed. Raheem's mother, Tasha, is a stripper and is rarely home, which is why Raheem basically took over their grandmother's house when she passed a few years ago. His father, Kareem, is in jail for life behind that wack-ass three-strikes law, leaving him and his little brother to fend for themselves. Raheem provides the best way he knows how: hustling weed and making beats.

The most striking feature of all of Raheem's fine qualities is his beautiful, black skin. Like onyx, it shines under the porch light. He's wearing a white wifebeater tee and baby blue Enyce sweats with his feet bare: There are no shoes allowed in his home. His tattoos serve as sleeves on his chiseled arms, complementing his narrow black eyes and angular face. I notice he has a new scribe directly under his father's name and date of entry into the penitentiary, complementing the scribe of a few verses from KRS One's song "Reality" and his mother's name on his other arm. I'll have to read the words another time. He's grown at least six inches, making him about six feet even now. The man looks like a Nubian pharaoh with a gangster twist.

"Jayd!" Kamal screams, running straight into me, almost knocking me down.

"Hey, lil man," I say, embracing his eight-year-old body. When Raheem and I were together, Kamal was in preschool and I treated him like my son.

"Are you still working up the hill at Simply Wholesome?" Kamal asks, nodding his head toward my job, which is within walking distance from here. Simply Wholesome isn't Raheem or Nigel's vibe: It's too pretentious. They much prefer Pann's chill atmosphere up La Cienega.

"Yes, I am."

"Did you bring me something to eat?" he asks, bringing back memories of sharing patties and burritos with him and his big brother, who's just staring at me through the doorway.

Finally, Raheem hangs up his phone and steps onto the porch, looking at me hard and making me even more nervous. I can smell his Egyptian Musk oil from the bottom of the porch steps. Nigel, noticing the vibe, walks up the porch steps past me to greet his homeboy.

"What's up, man? We ready to make them beats?" he says, breaking the ice.

"Yeah, man. We're ready." Raheem steps down to move Kamal out of the way before picking me up.

"Hey, Raheem," I say, completely engulfed in the best bear hug of my life. With my feet off the ground, I feel light as air in his arms. God, this man feels like heaven.

"Hey, Jayd," he says into my neck. His lips are still as smooth as Mama's shea butter. Why did I come here? I'm still weak for this man and that ain't good.

"Are you and my brother back together now?" Kamal says, tugging at my pants leg before Raheem releases me from his tight grip.

"Lil man, that's none of your business," I say. "But no, we're not." Raheem looks a little hurt by my definitive answer. But, I want to make sure everyone knows I'm no longer available to him or any other man, for that matter. Jeremy's the only man for me right now. And, after all the drama we've been through to be together in the past few weeks, I'm not giving him up for anyone. Least of all another ex.

"You look good. Smaller, but still as fine as ever," he says, first looking at my breasts, then the rest of me. "How you feeling?"

"I'm feeling fine. And, you're not looking so bad yourself. What did you do, take some growth pills or something?"

"Now you know being tall is in my DNA. It just took me a while to catch up," he says, directing Kamal into the house. Nigel and I follow right behind them.

"Alright, lil man. It's time for bed," Raheem says, ushering Kamal into the hallway toward the bedrooms.

"But, Rah, it's only ten. And, Jayd just got here," Kamal whines. "I haven't seen her since I was little."

"You're still little, which is why your ass has to go to bed, now. You're too young to hang with the big boys," he says, picking Kamal up in the air and throwing him over his shoulders like a sack of potatoes.

"Put me down. You don't want none of this, man!" Kamal screams, playfully hitting his brother's back.

"Say goodnight. And, I'm sure you'll see Jayd again soon," Raheem says, looking at me from the corner of his eye. Westingle brothas have no self-esteem issues. "Y'all make yourselves comfortable and I'll be right back."

As Nigel and I walk farther into the house, I see truly not much has changed. Directly ahead of us in the living room is still the same oversize cream leather couch with the huge aquarium right behind it. The big, flat-screen television is new, though.

"Jayd, you want something to drink?" Nigel says, walking through the dining room and into the kitchen, toward the bar. "You know Tasha keeps the house stocked with Hennessey," he says, taking two glasses out of the cupboard.

"Now you know I don't drink. But, I will take some water." Looking around, I notice it still looks like a party house. There are no family pictures around at all. Just fancy Black art on the walls, big tropical plants in every corner, and plenty of liquor.

Nigel puts a bottled water on the counter and I walk over to retrieve it.

"Alright y'all. Let's get this session started," Raheem says, coming in from the hallway and leading us through kitchen toward the garage. I step out of the living room, following them both.

"So, how's life treating you, Lyttle?" Raheem says, calling me by my former nickname. Nigel hands Raheem a glass of Hennessey and follows right behind me.

"Just fine. And, no one calls me that anymore," I say, passing him as he opens the back door leading to the converted garage. When I step inside, I'm stunned by how much work he's done in here. It no longer looks like a garage turned into a makeshift studio. It looks like a professional studio where the garage used to be.

"Damn, Rah. You've been hustling hard, huh?" I say.

"Me too, Jayd. We've been working hard up in here," Nigel says, taking a seat on the green, L-shaped couch along one wall. On the other side of the room is the producer's area, which has a turntable and a mixer damn near the length of the entire wall, several studio monitors, a subwoofer, and two sets of headphones and a microphone. There's also a desk with a leather executive chair, and two computers for his Pro Tools. On the wall behind the desk is a large shelf lined with CDs, tapes, and vinyl.

"You guys ain't playing at all about your shit," I say, impressed. Most brothas talk about making music but never invest in their art. These two spend every dime on their music, and it shows.

"Not at all. As a matter of fact, we're only two tracks away from our demo being finished and I plan on taking it to Atlanta with me next month. I want to see if some of Def Jam's people are interested. I was there over the summer and I ran a track by this DJ up there who says he's feeling our shit and got the hookup with some of Def Jam's people. So, we'll see what happens," Raheem says, setting his Hennessey down on his desk before taking a seat. "Alright, Nigel, get your punk ass in the booth and make our heads bop," he says, sounding like the Raheem I know and used to love.

"Damn, nigga, can't we chill for a minute? I ain't seen Lyttle—I mean, Jayd—in a couple of years. And, I know you want to catch up with her, don't you," he says, taking a blunt and some weed out of his pocket, ready to bless the session in their usual way.

"So, how's the White school, Jayd?" Raheem asks, taking a sip of his drink and fiddling with controls on his mixer. Some smooth tunes start to play through the sub woofers, mellowing the vibe in the room.

"It's real good, huh, Jayd?" Nigel says, ready to let all my business out. "She's holding it down, from what I hear."

"Shut up, Nigel," I say, pinching him in the arm before taking a seat next to him on the couch.

"I wouldn't expect anything less from you, girl," Raheem says, smiling in between sips. He looks at me as if he's undressing me with his eyes and reading my thoughts at the same time. His spirit is so strong. I swear he's been here a thousand times before.

"How's Westingle?" I say, changing the subject. I don't like being on the spot around Raheem. He can see straight through me, just like Mama. And, I don't want to tell him too much about my new relationship, knowing he'll dissect it and twist everything around, like he always does.

"It's cool. Better than that wack-ass Family Christian. I'm glad my mom let me transfer out, not that she had much of a choice," he says. "After my grandmother passed, there was no one to pay my tuition. And, my little brother needed me closer to his school anyway."

"How's your dad?" I ask, knowing he and his father are

very close, even though he's on lock down in Georgia for life.
I assume that's the real reason he's visiting Atlanta.

"He's cool, holding the Muslims down in there. You know
how he does it."

"But, back to the subject at hand," Nigel says, passing an
immaculately rolled blunt to Raheem who promptly lights it.
Smoke soon layers the air. "Did you know Jayd dips in vanilla?"

"Nigel," I say, slightly offended. Why did this fool have to
go and say something stupid shit like that?

"What the hell does that mean?" Raheem says, passing the
blunt to me. I shake my head a quick "no" and he passes it to
Nigel, who's just smiling and waiting for the argument. He
always did love to start shit between me and Raheem, which
isn't hard. Raheem thought he owned me and I am always
quick to let anyone know I'm my own woman.

"He's referring to my new man, Jeremy," I say, stealing
some of Nigel's thunder. "He's Jewish," I add, taking a sip of
my water while Raheem processes what I've just told him.
When he lived with his dad in Compton, we used to have
long, philosophical conversations about White folks, especially interracial dating. Raheem swore he would never date
a White girl. And I never even thought about dating a White
boy, until I met Jeremy.

"Really?" Raheem says. "A White, Jewish boy?" he asks, surprised. He takes another sip of his drink while Nigel passes
the blunt my way to give to Raheem. I rise slightly from my
seat and pass it to him, unofficially becoming part of the rotation.

"Do you know another kind of Jewish boy?" Nigel says,
sounding faded. Why did he have to bring this up now? I was
really looking forward to just vibing and being in the studio.
I get off on the process of making beats. It's so incredible,
the way they mix sounds to make an entire song. And, I love

the way Nigel rhymes. I know I'm going to see them at the Grammys one day.

"Well, Sammy Davis, Jr., was Jewish," I say, trying to lighten the mood.

"Yeah, but you ain't dating him. You're dating a rich White guy named Jeremy. And, he ain't related to no tap dancer," Nigel says. Damn, he's on it tonight.

"Is he treating you well?" Raheem asks, eyeing the gold bangle hanging from my wrist.

"Very," I answer, self-consciously turning the bangle to its upside, revealing the engraved *J* on its face.

"Well, that's all that matters, right, Jayd?" Raheem says, sounding sad yet sincere. "Let's get started, man. All cell phones off during session. It's getting late and I know you still have a curfew, don't you?" he says looking from Nigel to me before putting the blunt out and putting his headphones on.

"That's all you have to say?" Nigel says, surprised by Raheem's response. "I expected a showdown like old times. I'm very disappointed in you man," he says, rising from his spot and stepping into the booth.

"I got your letter. And, you can't be the same Rah," I say, also shocked by his chill attitude. Raheem looks at me like a wounded puppy before setting up the first track for Nigel to work on. I don't know what to make of Raheem's response. Is he disappointed in me, or in himself for letting me go in the first place? Whatever the case, I'm sure this is only the beginning of a new phase in our relationship.

"I hope you're happy Jayd," he says. "You just make sure he treats you like the queen you are, and nothing less." And with that, Rah starts the music.

~ 5 ~
Endgame

*"I can tolerate a still heart/
But I can't stand being alone."*

—CREE SUMMER

When I get home at one in the morning, I turn my phone on to see Jeremy left two voice messages and one text message. I feel guilty for not fully disclosing last night's plans, but I just didn't think he'd understand.

"Miss, did you here my order?" this rude ass regular says to me, snapping me back into work. I've been here all morning, but really my mind has been on Raheem and Jeremy all along.

"Oh, my bad. Yes, I got it: a veggie burger with everything except sprouts, lettuce, tomatoes, and cheese," I repeat, hoping he feels as stupid as he sounds.

"Don't forget the onions," he says looking at the menu like Shahid's added something new in the week since this man's last visit.

"You want onions?" I ask in a tone indicating I'm way past my tolerance level.

"No, no onions," he reiterates, carefully returning the menu to its holder on the counter.

"Well, then why did you say you wanted everything when in fact, you want it plain?" I ask, knowing I'm way over the line, but I can get away with it because we all do it from time to time. Working in customer service can be a bitch.

"Oh, I hadn't noticed. OK then, I'll have a veggie burger,

plain," he says, all proud like he just took his first step. Whatever. My mind's not here anyway. I just have to make it through the rest of my afternoon before my date with Jeremy tonight. I can't help but think about the story of Maman Marie and what Mama said about women's power in relationships. If that's true, how do I use my power in my relationship with Jeremy to get him to take me to the homecoming dance? 'Cause I can't be seen alone, especially not with Misty, Shae, and KJ going, not to mention my girls and their dates. I'll stick out like hot pink cornrows on a White girl, and a sistah can't have that.

When Jeremy gets to my mom's house, I invite him up to talk for a while before we head out for the evening. I figure if he gets too upset I can handle it here better than out in public.

"Hey, baby," I say, giving him a big hug and kiss before leading him to the couch.

"We better roll if we're going to catch the show at nine," he says. I don't want to be late either. I've wanted to see *Blood and Chocolate* for a while now. But, I've got to convince him to go to the dance with me. It's too important to let it go.

"We've got a little time," I say, sitting close to him, forcing him to smell my perfume and look into my eyes. In reading her story, I discovered using her seductive qualities to get men to listen to her was one of Maman Marie's tricks. And, she was very good at it. Maman had every man in Paris swooning after her, like Mama in New Orleans. I'll try to be a little sweeter than the last time Jeremy and I talked about this.

"Hey, Jeremy," I whisper.

"Yes, Jayd," he says, waiting to see what I'm up to. He's so cute when he looks at me like this. It makes me want to kiss his smile.

"Are you sure you can't go to the dance with me?" I say,

rubbing the inside of his thigh. "There will be a lot of dudes there and I don't want to be caught alone," I say.

"How did I know you were going to ask about the dance?" he says, stopping my hand with his and returning it to my leg. "I can't be bribed, Miss Jackson."

"I'm not trying to bribe you. I'm just showing you how much I value you," I say, gently pinning him down. Without much effort, Jeremy picks me up and makes me stand, laughing the entire time.

"You're so cute when you're feisty," he says, hugging me. "But, Jayd, I thought we discussed this. It has nothing to do with me not wanting to be with you. I told you I'll drop you off and pick you up. Go, have a good time. Be with your girls. It's Nellie's night anyway and you'd ignore me the whole time," he says, thinking he's reassuring me. But, I don't need reassuring. I need a man who'll be present in my life, at dances and all.

"Why do I feel like I'm being patronized?" I say, pushing him away from me and getting my jacket off the rack by the door.

"I'm not patronizing you," he says, coming up behind me and grabbing my waist. It will be hard to stay mad at him for long if he keeps touching me like this. He feels too damned good. But, not quite good enough to take away my swelling anger.

"Does this have something to do with Tania running for homecoming queen?" I ask, completely out of left field. According to Maman's story, this was also a bad habit of the Williams women—saying the first thing on our minds, no matter how wrong it may be.

"What? No, hell no. I couldn't care less about that girl, Jayd. Are you still jealous because she flirts with me in class, on the rare occasion she's there?" he says, still hugging me. "Come on, Jayd. Don't do this. It's been a long week and I just want to kick it with my girl, watch a movie and chill, since you blew me off last night to do your hair," he says, making me feel guilty.

"I'm not doing anything. You're the one who won't take his girl to the first party of the year and show me off, like a good boyfriend would," I say. He has to take me to the dance. It just doesn't make sense that he wouldn't want to. "Are you ashamed to be seen at a school event with me? You don't want people to know we're a serious couple? What is it, Jeremy? It can't just be because Reid's president of ASB and they're putting on the dance. That's just silly and immature," I say. I'm really pissed now. All my sweetness has flown out the door.

"Jayd, you're taking this way too far. And, for the record, you were the one who didn't want to be a serious couple until recently. Let's just go before we miss the movie. If you can't understand or simply respect the fact that I don't want to go, then fine. You'll either deal with it or not," he says, like a man used to getting his way. He reaches past me to open the door and steps outside waiting for me to follow.

If he thinks this conversation is over, he's got another thing coming. Maybe he's used to broads accepting his word as the law. But, not me. Another pervasive quality in my legacy is the ability to persist indefinitely. I'll just wait until after the movie to present my case again. He'll eventually bend. He just has to.

After the long, silent ride to the theater, we each soften a little and sit hand in hand through the entire movie as if nothing happened. But, I've been boiling inside the entire time, trying to figure out a way to get Jeremy to see the bigger picture. I have to speak his weird guy language in order to get him on my side. But how?

And, I still have yet to mention my studio adventures last night. I have to tell him before Monday. I'm sure Nigel will mention it at some point, which means Misty will hear, which means it'll be around school by the end of the day. Better to diffuse the situation before it turns into something bigger than it is.

"Jeremy, do you play chess?" I ask as we walk out of the Marina Theater's lot and toward the shopping area. It's ten p.m. and people are hanging out all over the brightly lit outdoor mall.

"Yes, I do. My brothers and I have been playing for years," he says.

"Really?" I say, planning my next move. "So, what's your favorite piece?" I ask.

"I would have to say the queen," he says, holding me tight as we walk around, window shopping.

"I knew you would say that," I say, stopping in front of a store with my ideal homecoming dress. This must be a sign.

"Why do you think I like the queen so much?" he says, following my eyes down the full length of the red halter gown. With my gold Steve Madden heels and Jeremy by my side, this would complete my homecoming vision.

"Because she can move in any direction, giving her the most maneuverability on the board," I reply, leading him into the store to watch me try on the dream dress.

"Well, that's true. But, it's not the main reason I like her so much." As he breaks down his chess philosophy, I pick out a size seven and pull it off the rack. I notice the price is way out of my league, but I'm used to dreaming big. I know I can't afford it, but I still want to try it on.

"Are you listening to me?" he says, smiling at me as I lead him into the dressing room area to sit in a waiting chair.

"Yes, of course I am," I say, stepping into an empty dressing room and slipping out of my clothes.

"Do you need any help?" a sales lady asks from behind the closed door.

"No, we're fine," I answer, eyeing myself in the mirror. I'm so glad I got a breast reduction last year. Otherwise, wearing a dress like this would be out of the question.

"Roses," says a man's voice. It's one of the dudes that follow all the couples around the mall with overpriced roses. Neither of us responds and I want to hear the rest of Jeremy's comment.

"Please continue, Mr. Weiner," I say while pulling the dress over my head without messing up my braids.

"I like the queen because even as powerful as she is, she's still willing to sacrifice herself for the king's life. Because in the end, she knows that's more important than her ability to move all over the board," he says, defeating my strategy once and for all. The boy read my mind without any effort. He must be a really good chess player, as good as he is at seeing three steps ahead of my psychological moves.

"Are you coming out or do I have to come in to see how it looks on you?" he says. I don't want him to see the defeat on my face. But, I do look damn good in this dress.

"Come on, let me see, pouty lips and all," he says, making me chuckle. He's right. It doesn't matter what other people may think of us. What matters is that we have fun together and we're a good match.

I open the door to find Jeremy sitting there with a long-stemmed yellow rose, looking like my prince charming in raggedy Birkenstocks. He's so sweet to buy me a flower while I was in the dressing room, even if he's being stubborn about the dance.

"Damn," he says for lack a better response, I suppose.

"I agree," I say, taking the yellow flower from his hand and putting it up to my nose. He bends down and kisses me passionately, just like our first kiss at the beach. Some sacrifice is always necessary in relationships, no matter what part you play. And, I guess my sacrifice for this lovely man is the public image of a perfect couple. Well, judging from my past with KJ and Raheem and the past of my ancestors, the lesson to be learned from this sacrifice is, quite possibly, how to be in a happy relationship.

After three more hours of making out, Jeremy finally drops me back off at my mom's. I never find the nerve to tell him about last night's session. I don't want to risk ruining our calm vibe after regaining a good momentum from the tension about homecoming. Maybe I can get Nigel to keep his mouth shut, although I doubt it. Mickey already told me he knows some other folk up at South Bay, though she said he didn't drop any names. I'll have to holla at him tomorrow at some point and see if we know any more of the same people.

I'm coming for that number one spot, Luda announces a very late-night phone call. Maybe it's Nellie calling to see how my date was. But when I look at the caller ID I see it's not her. It's Raheem.

"Hello," I say, sitting straight up on my makeshift bed. My mom's in her room sound asleep, so I don't have to worry about waking her up.

"What's up girl?" Raheem says. "Did I wake you?" he asks. I can hear low music in the background: tonight's session must be ending.

"I just got home a little while ago. So, I wasn't quite sleeping yet," I answer. "What's up?" I ask. I remember looking forward to weekends at my mom's so we could stay on the phone late. She never tripped like Mama does. He hasn't called me late at night in years. Well, he hasn't called me at all in years. So, he must have something on his mind.

"So, how's the White boy?" he asks, with a slight smile in his voice. I miss our extended phone conversations. Before my cell days, he would call me after school and we'd stay on the phone until my uncle Bryan came home and demanded I get off his line. He's the only one in the house with a personal line, other than Mama. She basically uses the main phone line for herself since she's the only one in the house without a cell. And, as long as I kept quiet and to myself, she didn't bother me too much until Bryan got home.

"He's good," I say, knowing he doesn't really care. I've been down this road with Raheem before. He always feels remorseful for treating me like shit for so long when he sees me with someone else. And, I used to fall for his act every time. Maybe that's why my daddy stopped paying for me to go to Family Christian. After all the madness with my cousin Nia, I guess he wanted Raheem out of both of our lives. But, after we made up and Raheem kicked Nia to the curb, I wouldn't budge from his side. We were together for another year and a half after that, until I came to Drama High.

"Jayd, what the hell is wrong with you?" he asks, getting straight to the point. This is the Raheem Nigel was missing last night. "A White boy? Now, I know you may be missing a nigga, baby. But don't go getting all desperate and shit, Jayd. You could've just picked up the phone and called me," he says, amusing himself with his witty hood repartee. At times, he sounds a bit like KJ. But, unlike KJ, Raheem wears his confidence like a crown and it's very seductive.

"I'm not desperate, Raheem," I say. "I'm happy. Do you know what that is?" I ask. "That's when a dude spoils me and doesn't cheat on me and makes me laugh and challenges my mind," I say, listing all of Jeremy's good qualities, like I'm his character witness.

"Yeah, but can he make your soul move?" Raheem says, making me remember Jeremy doesn't believe in God, or a soul, I assume. Raheem and I used to have long, deep discussions about all the different religions in the world, especially among Black folks. And whenever he came over, he and

Mama would vibe for hours about traditional religion and Mama's role in it. Mama actually likes Raheem as a person. It's his actions she doesn't care for.

"My soul doesn't need moving," I say, not wanting to get into a deep conversation with him right now. It's almost two in the morning and I have to get up and go to work in a few hours. Besides, I shouldn't be on the phone with him at all. He doesn't understand what it means to be just friends.

"Jayd, this is Rah, your boy from way, way back in the day. What happened to my little revolutionary, spunky street scholar?" he says, referring to our old crew. "She'd never be seen with no White dude," he says, sounding genuinely disappointed. Not just hating, like KJ.

"Well, things change," I say, feeling a little guilty. What the hell? "And, I got to get up and go to work in the morning, Mr. Super Producer," I say, trying to get off the phone. "Thanks for the shout-out," I say, ready to push "end."

"Wait, Jayd," he says. "You looked good last night. And, I don't mean just in the physical." Oh, here we go.

"Rah, I don't have time for this," I plead. He has the same kind of power over me that Mama's daddy had over her mother, and my father had over my mother. It's best I end this conversation right here, right now.

"Jayd, you're glowing," he says, ignoring my plea. "I remember when you first told me you were getting a breast reduction. I didn't want you to. But, now look at you. I don't know if it's from the surgery, the new man or what. But, you shine, girl. And, I just wanted you to know I see you. I see you," he says, making me stop and listen to every word. Why does this conversation feel so familiar?

"I must've been insane to treat you the way I did," he says. "And, I don't want to make your life difficult or no shit like that. But, I miss you in my life. Can we start over, as friends?" he says, sounding sincere. Truth be told, I miss him too. I never stopped missing him. Part of the reason I fell so easily for KJ in the first place was because he was the closest thing at school I'd seen to Raheem.

"I don't know, Rah," I say, not sure what to do. "You're not good at being my friend."

"I will be this time," he says, not giving up. "I'll even introduce myself at homecoming when I see y'all," he says, catching me off guard.

"Whose homecoming?" I ask.

"Yours," he says. "You think I'm going to miss my boy's premiere game? I got money riding on him, baby," he says. I forget he's a betting man. He used to play craps behind the boy's locker room in junior high. And, he usually won.

"Well, Jeremy won't be there," I say, still feeling the pinch of this evening's disagreement.

"Why the hell not? The boy ain't got no school spirit?" he asks. Westingle brothas take school functions very seriously. Raheem went to every event at Family Christian, with me right by his side. And, I'm sure he hasn't missed any at Westingle, either. The boys and girls there alike take pride in getting all pimped out for special occasions, cars and all.

"He's just not into school events," I say, not understanding Jeremy's issues myself. But, like he said earlier, I'll either deal with them or not. And, right now, I choose to deal.

"Not even if you are? Now, that ain't right," he says. "If you were still my queen, I wouldn't let you out of my sight for a minute. I know you gone look fine, girl," he says. I would if I'd get the dress I tried on earlier. Why am I still on the phone with this boy? He ain't doing nothing but bringing up bad feelings.

"Well, I'm not your queen. So, it's no longer your concern. Now, for real. I got to go, Raheem. Good night," I say, but hanging on his final good-bye.

"You'll always be my queen." And, with that last move, he hangs up. I sulk myself to sleep.

~ 6 ~
Reality Sucks

"My cow just died/
I don't need your bull."

—SALT 'N' PEPA

"So, how was your date last night, Miss Thang?" Sarah asks, smacking me on my behind with a towel. I love working with her on the weekends. She makes the time go by much faster.

"It was all right," I say, not really wanting to get into a deep conversation right now. It's one o'clock and the after-church crowd will be here any minute.

"That doesn't sound like a good time to me," she says in a strong, Jamaican accent. This girl is straight out of Kingston. Only seventeen years old, she helps support her mother, little sister, and two little brothers. She's in school full-time at Crenshaw High, graduating this year. "Come on and tell Auntie Sarah all about it," she says, laughing. She can be so crazy sometimes.

"No, nothing bad happened. And we did have a good time, for your information," I say, retrieving the wet towel from the juice sink and smacking her in the arm with it.

"Hey, you were supposed to work out all of that frustration on your date last night, remember? I guess it didn't go so well after all, huh, lady?" she says taking the oversize blender full of juice and pouring it into the large Styrofoam cup, making me thirsty.

"What kind of smoothie is that?" I ask, reaching for my own cup to pour myself a sample.

"The kind you can't have none of until you tell me what happened on your date last night that's got you so tense," she says. "Here. Give this to that man when I call his name. Me not want to see him right now," she says, referring to the same regular from yesterday who made my butt twitch with his plain veggie burger.

"I don't want to see him either," I retort as she calls his name through the microphone. "Besides, he's your customer," I say, forcing the large drink back into her hands and returning to the blender for my free sample.

"Did someone call Gerald?" he asks, pretending he didn't hear her. He was sitting right by the door next to the counter where we are. Customers can be so strange sometimes.

"Yeah. Here's your shake. Have a nice day," Sarah says half-heartedly, rushing from the counter to the kitchen in the back.

As I pour the banana, mango, peach, and wheat germ smoothie into my small cup, I hear Gerald utter a sigh of disgust. "Excuse me, miss. Is that my smoothie you're drinking?" Gerald asks me as I take a sip of the thick shake. Sarah sure can mix a drink.

"No. Your smoothie's in that cup," I say pointing to the drink in his hand. "This here is what we like to call leftovers."

"Yeah, but at Jamba Juice they give you your leftovers," he says, expecting an apology or something of the sort.

"Well, I hear they closed down Fat Burger and opened one next to Magic's Starbucks in the Ladera Center," I say, leaning up against the counter, sipping my drink. He's really got his nerve, demanding more after all the shit he puts us through on a regular basis. And today, I'm just not in the mood.

"With that attitude, young lady, you'll never get ahead," he says as he turns around and walks out the door.

"Good job, girl. I don't know what Jeremy did to get you all riled up, but I'm glad I'm not at the receiving end of your wrath today," Sarah says, coming through the swinging doors that connect the front counter area to the kitchen.

"God, he's pretentious," I say, still irritated at Gerald's audacity. Luckily Shahid wasn't here. I would have received the lecture of my life if he witnessed that little episode. "I'm not all riled up. There's just a lot on my mind today."

"All right, Jayd. Stop making me wait and just tell me what's going on with you and your man," Sarah says, perching herself up against the counter, ready to listen.

"It's really kind of silly, especially since usually I'm not really into dances. But, my girl Nellie is running for junior class homecoming princess and I want him to be my date, but he's not into dances."

"So, take someone else. That's what I would do in your situation. That'll teach him to take you the next time around."

"I can't do that. It would be rude."

"Why? Your man doesn't want to go, so that must mean he's cool with you having another date. Or at least that's the way I'd take it if I were you. And what's rude is your boyfriend not wanting to take you and show you off, no matter how much he hates dances."

As Sarah cleans the front counter, I decide to rearrange the desserts in the display case, thinking about what she just said. Maybe I should go to the dance with someone else. Just because Jeremy doesn't want to go doesn't mean I should go alone.

"You know what, Sarah? You've got a good point," I say, shifting my weight from one foot to the other, finishing my smoothie.

"A good point about what?" Summer, our manager, asks as she walks in from the store to the restaurant, surprising both of us.

"Jayd's man doesn't want to go to the homecoming dance and Jayd wants to go," Sarah says, making my monumental problem sound so simple.

"I know you're not letting some man control you, Jayd," Summer asks, replacing the menus left on the tables to their holder on the counter. "Once you let them control one decision, they'll take that as the cue to control them all." Summer's a trip. Forty years old and never married, she's got two kids, both in college. Short and tiny with locks to her butt, the sistah's real strong in her opinions and lets everyone know it. She also doesn't take any shit. That's why she and Shahid make the perfect management team.

Summer's got a good point. There's always some madness when dealing with men. It's better I get this mess with Jeremy out of the way sooner than later.

"Summer, can I take a quick break?" I ask, walking toward the counter, assuming she'll say yes. It's cool like that here.

"Sure, but make it quick. You know the church folk will be here any minute," she says, walking to the back to change the Bob Marley CD now playing to one of Aretha Franklin's gospel albums, our Sunday favorites.

"Going to talk to your White boy?" Sarah asks while cleaning out the blender.

"Yeah. I want to see if he'll mind me going to the dance with someone else," I say, knowing I'm about to start something. But, Summer's right and so is Sarah. I can't let him keep me from enjoying myself. If I can't have my dress, I will have my fun.

"Hello," Jeremy says, sounding like he was in the middle of a good nap. It must be nice to sleep the afternoon away.

"Hey, baby," I say. "Got a minute?"

"Yeah, what's up?" he asks, waking up. "You need a ride home?" he asks, remembering it's my day to go back to Mama's.

"No, my mom's going to take me. I wanted to ask you

something else," I say, almost ready to back out. But, Sarah steps outside to where I'm standing by the front entrance, signaling for me to go through with it.

"What's on your mind?" he says, now fully awake.

"Would it bother you if I went to the dance with someone else?" I ask.

"Not at all," he says. I thought he'd be a little surprised, pissed, something. This boy's nonchalance never ceases to amaze me. "You're your own woman."

"OK, cool. I just thought I'd let you know I'm considering it," I say, now seriously thinking about taking someone else, since he's calling my bluff.

"I'm cool with it, Jayd. I think you should have a good time. And, I'm not concerned about you being with any other guys. I trust you," he says. God, he's good.

"Fine," I say, watching the church procession pull into the parking lot. "I've got to go back to work now. I'll see you in the morning," I say, rushing off the phone. He's put me in a very awkward position. Now I'll have to find someone to go with just because I said I would. If I don't, he'll never fall for another one of my bluffs again.

It's hard enough to come home from my mom's cozy, feminine apartment to Mama's house full of men, but this evening's especially difficult and foul.

"Jayd, go on and tell Mama and Daddy I said hi. I'm already running late for dinner with Ras Joe," my Mom says, rushing me out of her car.

"All right, Mom. I'll see you Friday," I say, leaning over to kiss her on the cheek before getting out of her little Mazda. After retrieving my bags from the trunk, I walk through the back gate to find Lexi sleeping in her usual spot at the bottom of the porch steps.

"Hey, girl. Did you miss me?" I ask, stepping over her and onto the porch. As I enter the kitchen, the stench of a thousand funky asses hits me like a ton of bricks.

"What the hell is that smell?" I ask aloud to anyone who can hear me.

"The toilet overflowed and flooded the bathroom and hallway. Watch your step," Jay says, closing the refrigerator door. His face is masked against the smell.

"Is that my scarf?" I ask.

"Yes. It was the only one I could find. I'm sure you have plenty more, little miss thugette."

"Shut up and give it here. That's my pink, silk Coach scarf from last spring's collection!" I yell, snatching it from his face. "Why were you going through my stuff anyway?" I ask, following him from the kitchen and into the living room, where the stench worsens.

"I was saving your shit, man. Some of the water seeped into the closet where our stuff is. Damn. It's going to take forever to clear the smell out of the house," Jay says, taking a seat on the plastic-covered sofa before digging into his home-made burger and fries. Nothing stops these dudes around here from eating, not even the smell of a sewer in our house.

"Where's Mama?" I ask, not wanting to stay indoors any longer. And, knowing Mama, she probably went to a neighbor's house or Netta's.

"She's out back working off some steam. You missed it. Her and daddy had it out," Jay says, smacking his lips in between bites. "Daddy went back to the church for evening service. I don't know how he's going to preach about being holy after what he said to Mama and what she said to him."

"Jay, you act like they've never argued before," I say as I take my bags into the dining room and place them behind the china cabinet. "Make sure nobody touches my stuff and that includes you, sticky fingers," I say, heading through the kitchen and out the back door to find Mama. I need some good advice and now.

When I get outside, I can hear Mama humming to herself in the back. I go all the way around the garage toward the spirit room. Her and Daddy must've had a real good falling out to make her hum.

"Hi, Mama," I say, walking over to where she's kneeling by her herb garden, next to the backhouse. She's busy pulling weeds and picking fresh herbs.

"Hey, baby. How's your Mom?" she asks, turning her cheek up to receive my kiss. I kneel down beside her, gathering the extracted weeds to eventually toss into the garbage can.

"She's fine. Rushing off to meet Ras Joe," I say, thinking about my mom's crazy behind. I didn't even get a chance to mention my drama; she was so busy telling me about hers. She wants to call it quits with Ras Joe because he's getting too possessive. Her problem's the exact opposite of mine, as usual.

"That girl. When will she learn to leave those trifling men alone?" Mama says, tugging at the stubborn weeds a bit harder than necessary.

"Everything all right, Mama?" I ask. "Jay said you and Daddy had a fight."

"That old Negro thinks he can just do what he wants, when he wants," she says, going right into the drama. "I told him to call a plumber hours ago. But, no, he thinks he can fix the damn toilet his own self. He's cheap, Jayd. Just cheap," she says, ripping the weeds from the ground. "Now the hall's soaked with shitty water and the house smells like a sewer." I feel sorry for Mama sometimes. It must be hard being the matriarch in a house full of men.

"I'll help you clean up," I offer.

"Oh, no you won't either," Mama says, pulling the last of

the weeds and looking at me. Despite the anger apparent on her face, she looks at me gently and smiles.

"This is your grandfather's mess. Let him figure out a way to clean it up," she says. "Now, how was your weekend?" she asks, reminding me of my original intention.

"It was kind of cool, and it kind of sucked," I say. "Jeremy won't take me to homecoming and Raheem wants to be friends," I say, making it short and sweet.

"Well, you can still go to the dance, but not with Raheem, if that's what you're thinking." How did she read my thoughts before I even realized them myself?

"No, of course not," I say, shutting down the possibility. "But, Raheem did say he's going to be there."

"Did you find out what he wants?" she asks, searching for the truth in my eyes.

"He says he just wants to be friends," I say, knowing myself that can't be all. He wants me back and I'd be a fool not to admit it. What else could he have meant by saying I would always be his queen?

"Girl, you'd better be careful," Mama says, getting up from the ground and dusting off her outside work dress. "You've got two very powerful men after your heart," she says. "The last thing you want to do is pit the two of them against each other," she says, turning around and walking toward the house. "I recommend you find someone more amicable to go with. That way, you'll keep both of them at bay and yourself out the line of fire," she says before retiring for the evening.

Mama's right about one thing for sure. I don't want to pit them against one another. That's what happened with KJ and Jeremy, and that ended up really bad. I have to be careful with both of them. But, right now I have to do the crapload of homework I've put off all weekend before going to bed. The drama just never stops.

* * *

As I step out the door wearing my perfect red dress, a man's hand grabs mine, leading me onto the dance floor. The smooth sounds of Dexter Gordon play in the background, providing the beat to our one-two sway.

As we glide across the dance floor, with other couples in tune with the beat as well, he comes to a halt, dipping me back, and then pulling me up slowly into a breathtaking, deep kiss. When I pull back to look my dance partner in the eyes, they're familiar and powerful, but not belonging to whom I expect.

"Jayd, you want me to boil you some water?" Bryan says, reminding me the bathroom's off-limits this morning and I'll have to wash up in the kitchen sink. I went over to our neighbor's house last night to take a shower.

What the hell am I doing dreaming about Raheem? This isn't getting any better, and I'm sure today's just going to get worse. I have to get to Nigel before Misty gets wind of it, or else this thing with Raheem could get bigger than it needs to.

~ 7 ~
Misery Loves Company

"You busy smilin', smilin', grinnin' in my face/
Whole time tryna take my place."

—ANGIE STONE

It's the week before homecoming and people are naturally starting to set up their dates for the dance. It's weird having a boyfriend and no date. And, not only do I have a boyfriend; he's the most popular cat up here. So, how can any date I choose top him? Because of yesterday's at-home excitement, I wasn't able to call my girls last night and tell them the news. I know Nellie's going to flip when I tell her Jeremy's not taking me to the dance.

It was hard getting dressed in the kitchen this morning. It's cold as hell in there and there's no mirror. I kept running back and forth between the kitchen for the sink, the living room for the heat, and the dining room for the mirror. It's actually a relief to ride on the bus this morning. The house is still a mess and I'm glad I'm not on the clean-up crew for today. I'm sure I'll have enough shit shoveling to do once I hit campus.

When I finally reach school, Jeremy's waiting for me at the bus stop like clockwork. One good thing about him is he sure is punctual.

"Good morning, Lady J," he says, reaching over the passenger's seat and pushing the door open for me to get in.

"How are you this morning?" I say, throwing my backpack in the backseat before getting in. Neither one of us tries to kiss the other. I guess he feels the tension in the car as much as I do. Why do relationships have to be so hard?

"So, how was your night?" Jeremy asks, making small talk. At least he's making an effort. I really don't have anything else to say to him unless he's changed his mind. Otherwise, I need to concentrate on getting a date and fast.

"I did homework all night," I say, leaving out the gory details of my evening. I doubt he'd understand what it means to have the only bathroom in a house full of people break down, since there are five bathrooms in his house. "What about you?" I ask as he pulls into the parking lot.

"It was cool. I had an English paper to write for Mrs. Bennett. So, I was up all night working too," he says. "Jayd, are we cool?" he asks, taking the key out of the ignition and turning to give me his full attention.

"Sure we are, aren't we?" I answer. I want him to feel bad for leaving me hanging like this, but I don't want to go too far.

"I'm definitely cool. You're the one with the attitude," he says, opening the car door and getting out.

"Did you just roll your eyes at me?" I ask, getting out with as much attitude as he's accused me of having.

"Whatever, Jayd. I'm just trying to break the ice without all the mind games," he says. People are rushing up the steps to campus, paying no attention to our spat.

"What mind games?" I ask, knowing exactly what he's talking about. Maman Marie's ways are not proving to be too successful for me. Well, I guess they weren't all that successful for her either. This is what I get for trying to act after reading only half her story.

"You know what games," he says, getting both our backpacks out of the backseat and closing the car door. "All this noise about you going with someone else," he says, walking toward the stairs ahead of me. "You just said that to get a rise out of me," he says, walking backward to face me. He looks so adorable when he thinks he's got me.

"Oh, Jeremy," I say, catching up to him and pushing him, making him slightly lose his footing. "I am going to the dance with someone else. So, you can keep your chauffeur service to yourself. I won't need it or you," I say, not giving in to what he thinks he knows.

"All right, Lady J. We'll see when the night comes. Just remember, there are no hard feelings on my end. And, if you need me I'm there for you," he says, smiling like he's won the battle. But, the war has just begun.

When we get up to campus, Jeremy walks me to my locker and we go our separate ways. My girls aren't here yet. Maybe there's traffic on the 91 or something. I try calling Nigel, but his voice mail's picking up. Maybe he can take me to the dance. He's neutral enough and he's the star quarterback, definitely a good runner-up to Jeremy. I also need Nigel to keep his mouth shut about our late-night session. I don't see why my at-home life has to mingle with my life at school any more than it already does. I just hope I can get Nigel to see it my way.

When the bell for break rings, I bolt out of English class to find Nellie and Mickey and look for Nigel as well. South Central is closer to the English hall than my locker, so I figure I can save time by checking there first. Luckily, my girls are already posted at their usual spot, by the vending machines.

"Wait just a minute, Jayd," Nellie says, adjusting to my very unpleasant news. "You mean to tell me you're dating one of the most popular dudes up here and he's not into dances?

What's the point of having a man at all if he can't even take you to a school dance?" she says, sounding hella pissed.

"That's not why I'm with him, Nellie," I say, opening my bottled water and taking a sip. It's too hot to be out here defending myself against my girls. I wanted help, not more aggravation.

"Well, then why are you dating him, because I don't understand the purpose. Y'all seem to be a perfectly mixed match couple," Mickey says, smacking on some hot Poli Seeds, making me wish I had a bag myself.

"Speaking of which, here comes the oddest couple of them all." The only two people I see coming over our way are Misty and KJ, and I know Nellie can't be talking about them. A couple?

"Nellie, who are you referring to?" She and Mickey exchange a look that tells me I'm the one way out of the loop.

"Oh, you haven't heard," Nellie says. "Misty asked KJ to homecoming and he said yes," she says, passing me a Kleenex from her purse as if I'm about to let loose a flood of tears.

"What!" I exclaim with more emotion than I expected. "Just last week he was running from the broad. Now they're going to the first major dance of the year together? What the hell?"

"Why do you care? You chose Jeremy over him, remember?" Nellie says, violating our verbal agreement. But, she's got a good point. Why do I care? I should be happy for them. They deserve each other. But, I don't need Nellie rubbing it in my face.

"What happened to you not giving me any lip due to the fact I'm sacrificing my time and energy managing your princess campaign?" I retort, looking past Nellie to KJ and Misty approaching us. He does look nice today, as usual. I can only imagine how good he's going to look at the dance.

The whole point of going is to dress up with the ones you love, or love to hang out with.

"Maybe you should've waited until after the dance to break up with KJ," Mickey says, rubbing salt into my wounded pride.

"Shut up Mickey," I respond as KJ approaches us. But, true, we would have made a lovely homecoming picture.

"Hey, Jayd. How's the White boy?" KJ asks, with his hackling hen right by his side.

"He's just fine, KJ. Thanks for asking," I reluctantly answer. KJ's exceptionally cocky this morning and smiling way too big and bright. I know he's only taking Misty to the dance to piss me off. What an ass.

"I hope you don't mind us going to the dance together," Misty says, practically gushing with joy. "I heard you don't have a date yourself, being that the Weiner boys are known for not going to dances. You really should've done your research before dating one of them." She knows too much of everyone's business and I know this heffa's not trying to rub some shit in.

"You're a trifling little bitch, you know that, Misty?" Mickey says. "You have absolutely no shame in dating Jayd's leftovers, do you?" she says, looking Misty up and down like she's ready to throw blows on her. "No offense, KJ," Mickey says, not meaning to burn bridges with him. It's Misty she's after this morning.

"Whatever, Mickey. Is your man bringing you, or does his anklet only allow him to go to work and back?" Misty retorts, setting Mickey way the hell off.

"You know what, Misty? I've had about enough of your petty little games. I should've whipped your ass better when I had the chance," Mickey says, putting her bag of Poli Seeds in her purse and handing it to a shocked Nellie. I'm just waiting to see what's going to happen next.

"OK, you two. That's enough," Nellie says. "Y'all are caus-ing negative attention and I have a crown to win. And, we all want me to win, right?" Nellie can be so full of herself some-times. But, she's right. We are causing an embarrassing scene.

"Not that I agree with any of y'all right about now," I say, briefly recovering from the shock of Misty's dream coming true. "But, we need to chill. It's just not that serious," I say, even though I know it is that serious. How can a person who does so much foul shit get a date with my ex?

"Jayd, you need to check this trick," Mickey says, retriev-ing her purse from Nellie. "Some people never learn their lesson without a full beat-down. Later, KJ," Mickey says as she stands to go, leaving Nellie and me to deal with Misty and KJ.

"KJ, I would've gone to the dance with you if I'd known you were that desperate," Nellie says, biting into Misty in her own way.

"OK, catty ladies. Really, it's just a dance. We're not a couple or anything," KJ says, instantly wiping the smile off Misty's face.

"Whatever, KJ. We know dudes got a thing for overly large asses," I say, feeling a little relief after letting that one slip. Misty, like most of us, uses whatever assets she's got to get a man. And, lucky for her she's got that cute, thick J Lo thing going on. But, her attitude is what keeps her eternally single.

"Don't hate, Jayd. If you were with a Black man, you'd under-stand the true value of all of this," she says, outlining her voluptuous body, before turning her head, ponytail in tow, and walking across the courtyard to the cafeteria. KJ, enjoy-ing the show and Misty's departure, turns back to Nellie and me, but we've both had enough of this scene.

"KJ, what are you thinking going to the dance with her?" I say, ready to explode. I'm sick of the drama this brotha carries with him. And, most of all, I hate that I'm still involved in it.

"Why are you worried about who I go to the dance with?" he asks, obviously pleased with my reaction. He then leans up against the vending machine, in between Nellie and me. The games never end with KJ.

"I'm not worried about it," I say, wishing he'd back up off me. For some reason, his cologne's bothering me this morning, making me want to sneeze. "But, Misty?"

"But, Jeremy?" he says, mocking me. Nellie's getting a kick out of me sweating. "And, what's this I hear about him not taking you to the dance?" How does Misty get her information so quickly? That girl's like Google for South Bay High.

"He's cool on dances and I respect that," I say, defending my man. It's one thing for me to criticize his decision. But, it's an entirely different situation when someone else does it, especially KJ. "Besides, I've got another date," I say.

"Oh, really?" KJ says, stepping back to look at me lie to his face. "And, who might this other man be?" KJ asks. Right on cue, Nigel walks up to the courtyard, heading straight for us. Thank God.

"Here he comes now," I say, quickly leaving the vending machines to meet Nigel halfway. He doesn't know he's my date yet. But, first things first. I have to make sure he keeps his mouth shut about Friday night until further notice.

"What's up, Jayd?" he says, opening his arms to give me a hug. "Long time no see," he says, almost sharing the exact info I want him to keep on the low.

"What's up, man?" I say, walking right into his embrace. "Could you please not say anything about our session?" I whisper. I can feel everyone's eyes on us, especially KJ's.

"Consider it our little secret," Nigel whispers back, swaying me from side to side. I miss his hugs. He's always been a cool big brother, just like Chance. We untangle ourselves just in time for the warning bell. We hurry over to the vending machines to say a quick good-bye to my girl. KJ, who's now sitting, gets up as if he's about to leave, and that's just fine with me. I've had enough of him for today.

"Nigel, have you met my girl Nellie?" I ask, unsure if they've actually been introduced. I know he's met KJ, who shakes his head at me and nods a "what's up" to Nigel before heading off to class. I'm sure there was an unofficial meeting for the athletes on his first day here.

"No, not really. I just noticed her fine ass in class," he says, putting a smile on Nellie's face like only Nigel can. I told her there was something special about the brothas from Westingle. They're nothing if not bold about their shit because they have it like that. And Nigel, like most of the brothas up there, is fine. About 5'11" and built like he just got out the pen, he's a magnet for girls with any kind of attraction to an intelligent thug.

"Well, thank you," Nellie says. I think she's already sprung, with my safety date bouncing away right along with her.

"Alright, well I have to get to class," I say, feeling a little uncomfortable. They look like they want some privacy.

"Yeah, me too. Can I walk with you?" Nigel asks.

"Don't y'all want to vibe?" I say, stating the obvious. They really look taken with each other and I don't want Nellie to think I'm blocking. Besides, they're going to the same class.

"I'll see you in class, Nigel. And, nice to finally meet you," Nellie says, taking control of the situation. "I'll see you at lunch," Nellie says to me, still smiling, but a little less enthusiastically.

"Alright, Nellie," I say, going with the flow. Maybe Nigel wants to get the 411 on my girl before making a move. I lead Nigel in the direction of my government class, walking hella fast. All I need is to give Mrs. Peterson a reason to say something to me today. I can't deal with anymore archaic punishments like handwriting the constitution again.

"So, what's up with your girl?" Nigel asks, as predicted.

"Nothing. She's feeling you and y'all would make a cute

couple," I say, gently nudging him with my elbow. "You should holla," I say.

"I'm already part of a cute couple," he says, looking down at me and smiling slyly. That's another not-so-charming characteristic of Westingle brothas: They're dogs.

"Besides, I get the feeling she's a little stuck up. But, that other friend of yours is more my style," he says, referring to Mickey. She usually is most dudes' style: fine and unavailable. "What's up with her?" he asks, sounding like a kid in a candy store.

"Nigel, she's taken," I say, looking at him in disgust.

"So am I. My girlfriend's in college. We're perfect for each other." Now he's put me in an awkward position and I don't have the time to tell him off right now.

"I'll talk to you later, fool," I say, rounding the corner of the social science wing, where my government class is.

"Hey, Jayd, why the secret?" he asks, referring to our weekend rendezvous.

"Because, no one needs to know what I do on my off time," I say. I hope he understands.

Since I have to meet up with Nellie at lunch to make fliers, and Jeremy after school, I won't be able to talk to Ms. Toni until tomorrow morning. With all that's been going on, I haven't had a chance to fill her in on me and Nigel's association, Nellie's campaign, KJ and Misty going to the dance together, or Jeremy's avoidance of any function Reid throws. I need some school advice and she's the only one who can help me.

~ 8 ~
A History of Hatin'

*"You ain't a friend of mine/
You ain't no kin of mine."*

—50 CENT

It's only Tuesday and I'm already feeling the pressure of being Nellie's campaign manager. Reid has been on my jock hard since yesterday when he saw Nellie and I putting up posters around campus. We're also going to Kinko's tomorrow after school to make some buttons and pamphlets to pass out on Thursday. She's taking this campaign hella seriously, and I'm starting to catch her fire. It's a good diversion from the drama with Jeremy, though. Yesterday during government I asked him about the real beef between Reid's family and his family and he said it's ancient history. Well, if that's so, then Ms. Toni should know most of the details.

When I walk into the ASB office, I see homecoming crap all over the place. It's break and unusually crowded in here. The cheerleaders and athletes are sharing the ASB headquarters because both clubs are in charge of the homecoming festivities next week. Some are even rehearsing their performance routines for homecoming week in here. At their finger tips they have everything needed to run a successful campaign. Anyone associated with either of these cliques has a clear advantage for victory.

"Jayd, what a pleasant surprise," Reid says, looking prematurely triumphant, as usual. "Have you finally come to your senses and decided to rejoin the winning team?"

"I'm on the winning team. But, thanks for your concern," I say, passing Reid and his little helpers as I enter Ms. Toni's office, the calm away from the storm. It's so tranquil in her little hideaway at the back of the ASB room. She's even got an electric waterfall in the corner behind her desk. I just need a few minutes in her world to know everything in my world will be alright.

"Good morning, Ms. Toni," I say. She's seated behind her desk and I walk over to her for a hug. She's so thin I feel like I'm crushing her with my heavy backpack on my shoulder weighing me down.

"Have a seat and fill me in, girl," she says as I sit down in the chair across from her desk. "How's Nellie's campaign going?" she asks, offering me some cashews, which I accept. She always has the best snacks from Trader Joe's.

"Slowly, but we're picking up some steam," I say. "I'm her campaign manager."

"Really? And, that's OK with you? Being a campaign manager is just as political."

"I know. But, she promised to get off my case for the rest of the year. Not that I expect her to keep such a promise," I say, recollecting her recent slip ups. "But I can hold it over her head and that's priceless."

"Good reason to help your friend, Jayd," Ms. Toni says sarcastically. "What's she on your case about now?"

"Well, a couple of things actually. The main one is that Jeremy won't take me to the homecoming dance," I say, not surprising Ms. Toni at all.

"I thought you might be the one to get one of those boys to a dance after all," she says, a little amused at the turn of events. "But, I guess not."

"What am I missing here?" feeling like there's a common-knowledge story I missed the one day it was told.

"Girl, the Weiner and Connelly family feud goes way back before Jeremy and Reid," Ms. Toni says while separating the stack of paperwork on her constantly full desk. "I believe it started with the two older brothers over a girl, I'm sure."

"Why is it always over a girl?" I ask, already knowing the answer to that question.

"Well, I don't know all the ins and outs of what happened and when. But, I do know I've never seen any of them attend any school function, not even a football game."

"Really?" I ask, shocked at their devotion to a grudge.

"Really, Jayd. Those boys are serious as a heart attack about whatever went down between Michael and Ted, Reid's eldest brother," Ms. Toni says, offering me more nuts, which I gladly accept. The bathroom at home is still a slight mess and the kitchen has become a waste haven for everyone, not making it a pleasant place to eat breakfast.

"But, why carry it over into school functions? I just don't get it," I say. "This just all seems so insignificant, something you get over and talk about as a distant high school memory."

"Don't let Jeremy's aloof behavior fool you, Jayd. Those Weiner boys are very territorial. And, so are the Connelly brothers," she says, sounding as if she's warning me without knowing against exactly what. "You know Reid thinks of you as still a part of ASB, since you two made such a powerful debate couple and all, that is," Ms. Toni says, reminding me of my brief stint as an ASB member. Reid and I would go back and forth about all kinds of political hot topics: abortion, welfare, affirmative action. Whatever I was for, he was against. Not much has really changed between us, I guess.

"But that's insane," I say, rising with the ringing bell. We have a quiz in government this morning and I want a little time to look over our review questions before class begins. "I have no loyalty to ASB."

"Yes, and Reid does. He takes Nellie's campaign as a personal affront. And, the fact that you're dating his archrival doesn't help," Ms. Toni says, taking a sip from her coffee mug.

"Thanks for the warning," I say before heading out the door. I didn't get to tell her about Nigel. But, that can wait until another time.

What exactly happened between Michael and Ted, I wonder? I bet someone stole someone's girlfriend and the other person never got over it, or something like that. I guess I'll just have to ask Jeremy when we get a moment to chill. With Nellie's campaign taking off, I've been too busy for anything else, including my man or my spirit work.

Before I left this morning, Mama left a note on my jacket saying to meet her at Netta's after school and to bring my spirit notebook with me, which I forgot this morning. I know she wants to know if I read Maman Marie's entire story yet. I'm sure if I'd finished it, I'd know more of our own history of haters.

On my way home to retrieve my spirit notebook, I receive a text message from Raheem, saying he's missing my energy and hopes I can make it to the session this weekend. What am I going to say? I can't keep lying to Jeremy about my new Friday night habit, which I'm considering making permanent. I miss being around Rah and Nigel, not to mention the lil homey Kamal. But, I also don't want to rock me and Jeremy's already shaky boat. Maybe if I could bring him along once or twice, he wouldn't have a problem with me going. Rah and I can be friends, right?

When I approach the house, I can hear Bryan talking to someone on the porch. It's his cute friend from the radio station, Tarek. I like Tarek's whole vibe, especially the mellow tunes he kicks out on his show, Underground Bridge. Like Bryan's show, his theme is all about acknowledging the deeper roots of hip hop and Black folks in general.

"Hey, Jayd," Bryan says as I walk up the steps where

they're sitting, making sure Tarek catches my smile. He's way out of my league, yet I can't help but flirt.

"Hey, Bryan, Tarek. What brings you by?" I say, making small talk I don't have time for. I already know Mama's going to be pissed I left my notebook at home. I don't need to irritate her more by being late.

"Your uncle owes me some vinyl," Tarek says, meaning Bryan's habit of "borrowing" music. From what Bryan's told me, Tarek has an impressive collection. His weekly, two-hour radio spot only allows him to show it off a little. Tarek must have walls full of music at home.

What's hella bomb about Tarek is that he's not even from here. He was born in Libya and came here as a teenager. He's from a strict Muslim family, like Raheem. I love when he comes by. Too bad I can't chat longer today. I'm already late for my date with Mama and Netta.

"Well, I wish I could stay and talk, but I got to meet Mama at Netta's," I say, opening the front door and going straight to Mama's room, dropping my backpack on my bed and quickly retrieving my notebook before rushing back out.

"Send your grandmother my greetings," Tarek says as I pass by them by again and rush up the street.

"Will do. And, Tarek, I listen to your show every Tuesday," I say, walking backward to flash a final smile.

"I'll send out a special dedication for you next week," he smiles back as I head up Gunlock to Netta's Never Nappy Beauty Shop. Before I turn I catch Bryan shaking his head and grinning at my shameless flirting. That's one part of our legacy I've got down pact. It's everything else I'm not sure about.

When I get to the shop, Mama's already sitting in Netta's chair, getting her weekly french twist.

"Where the hell have you been?" Mama asks, impatient

with my tardiness, as anticipated. Netta's giving me a look
that says, "Jayd, you better have your assignment done or
your Mama's going to have your ass in a sling." Ever since
Daddy let the plumbing get backed up, Mama's been in a
foul mood. She gets like this from time to time, when it all
gets to be too much for her.

"I left my notebook at home," I say, knowing my negli-
gence will only infuriate her more. But, it's better than telling
her that Jeremy dropped me off a little late, and I had to take
a minute to flirt with Tarek.

"Well, you've got it now," Mama says as Netta cocks her
head to one side, a little rougher than necessary. She's a
good buffer from Mama's fire.

"Watch it, Netta," Mama says.

"Well, you need to calm down. You didn't even let the girl
get in the door good before laying into her," Netta said, defending me.

"Read me your notes from Maman's story," Mama says,
while Netta brushes and sprays Mama's smooth, black hair.
Noticing my extended silence, Mama looks up at me, completely vexed.

"Jayd, did you finish reading Maman's story?" Oh, shit.
Now I know I'm in for it. I've only read some parts here and
there, but not from beginning to end. Nor have I written
down any of the lessons I've learned so far.

"Well, I didn't know I needed to be finished with it by a
particular date," I say, trying to buy myself some sympathy.
But, Mama's not falling for the ignorant act this afternoon.

"Jayd, you know better than to play with me, girl," Mama
says, allowing Netta to continue her styling, although I can
tell Mama wants to jump out of her chair and choke me. I
reposition myself in my seat across from Netta and continue
with my excuses.

"Mama, with all that's going on at the house and school I

just haven't had time to read it. But, I have skimmed through and I'm learning a lot," I say.

"Skimmed through? Netta, did she just say she skimmed through my mother's history?" Mama asks, now looking me dead in my eyes. Netta's momentarily given up trying to control Mama's head. I have a feeling it's been like this, to some extent, all day long.

"I didn't mean it like that," I say, realizing I've hurt Mama's feelings. "But, I've been overwhelmed with Jeremy and Raheem."

"If I recall correctly, Jayd, reading Maman's legacy is a prescription to help you with your little boy troubles," she says. "You need to take your history more seriously, Jayd. Everything you need to help you in this life has already been lived and figured out in the lives lived before yours." Mama, looking somewhat defeated, relinquishes control of her head, again following Netta's lead.

"Well, some of the lessons I've learned have been helpful," I say, only vaguely recalling my readings. But, so far I've been falling right into Maman's downfall instead of learning from her mistakes.

"Without writing it down the only person you're hurting is you. Make sure and ask your Mama about the repercussions of doing half-assed work. And Jayd, I want my assignment sooner than later or you won't be going out with any of your little boyfriends for a long, long time," she says. With that kind of threat, I better make the best of this weekend. I'll just have to wait until Friday to talk to my mother about Mama's warning. She's never been this upset about me not finishing a lesson before.

Well, come hell or high water, I'll have it done by next weekend. If for no other reason, than to help me with this Raheem and Jeremy mess. I can still feel Raheem's lips from my dream about us kissing. Lord knows I don't want to go through no more drama with his ass. But, I do want to keep him around as a friend. He and Nigel are just cool peoples who've known me and loved me from way back. And, I don't want there to be any negative energy between Jeremy and them. I've already seen how Jeremy handles his enemies and I don't want him to have any more on my account.

After yesterday's drama with Mama, I've been walking on eggshells at home. As a diversion, I've decided to completely throw myself into Nellie's campaign. After school, the Drama Club will have a brief meeting to decide what to do with our performance day during next week's homecoming festivities. I'm glad Jeremy takes me to Compton every day. It gives me free time in the afternoons that would normally be spent on one of the three bus rides I would take home. And today, I'm in no rush to get home.

Finally deciding on a grassy spot outside the drama room to hold our meeting, Alia, Leslie, Matt, and Seth sit opposite me, Jeremy, Nellie, and Chance. Alia tries to hide her feelings for Chance by not sitting next to him. But, everyone knows she's got it bad for him. Too bad Chance is only interested in Nellie at the moment. He's let all his White girls fall to the side for now, hoping he can when Nellie's favor by spending more time with her during the campaign.

Nellie's the only homecoming princess candidate out of our four at the meeting. All of the candidates were chosen by Seth with Matt's approval. And, quite naturally, he picked only divas, like Tania and Nellie, to be our nominees. Normally, none of the candidates would be here. But, because she's my friend, no one minds her being present. Our meetings are much more laid back than ASB or any other club, I'm sure.

"So, what's the good word, people?" Matt says, officially calling the meeting to order in his own way. He's our president and Leslie's the secretary. We don't have any other officers because we don't need them. Mrs. Sinclair, our teacher and sponsor, keeps all of our money so there's no need for a treasurer, and who cares about the vice president anyway? "We've got twenty minutes, so let's get going. Leslie, are you writing this down?" Leslie's too busy puffing on her Marlboro Light to write anything down.

"I'll keep minutes," Alia says, pulling a composition notebook out of her backpack and turning to a fresh page.

"OK, good. So, who has a suggestion for our homecoming performance?" Matt asks, taking a hit from Leslie's cigarette.

"I think we should perform a spoof of the athletes and cheerleaders like we did last year. That guaranteed us popularity for the rest of the year." Seth's right about that. No one ever forgot how entertaining the Drama Club was last year, especially not the athletes and cheerleaders.

"Nah, man. We need to do something original and unexpected," Chance says, leaning back on the grass, allowing him a better view of Nellie's backside. Jeremy and I look at each other, sharing a giggle at Chance's expense.

"I don't understand how a performance is going to help me win," Nellie says, expertly shifting the focus of the meeting to her crown. "What we need is a campaign like Laura's."

"Would you please get off of Laura's jock for a minute and let us do our thang?" I say, tired of her wanting to be something she's not. "We get votes by getting the masses on our side. And we do that by performing, not just by passing out fliers and pamphlets about how great you or the other candidates are," I say, making everyone in the group smile, except for Nellie.

"This is what we need, right here," Chance says. Matt and Jeremy nod in agreement. "This is our skit."

"What the hell are you talking about?" I ask.

"This, right here. We need to put together a scene with you two clowning the ASB's campaign and then we follow it up by a song or some shit," Matt says, rising from his spot on the grass and walking around our circle.

"Yeah, like the two of them talking about the posters and all the sweating her punk ass boyfriend Reid's doing on her behalf," Chance says. "And then we can have a rap song to top it off. This is going to be hilarious," he says, reassuring Nellie, who looks like her worst fears have just come true.

"It all sounds great, but I don't want to perform," Nellie says. "That's your department, Jayd. I don't want people to see me on stage until I'm being crowned," she says, reclaiming her position as the diva of the group.

"Whatever," I say, tiring of her attitude.

"That's fine. We can get Chance to do it," Matt says. "You two were going at it during my party a few weeks back. If you can bring that same spark to the stage, which we all know you can, we've got it made." Jeremy, looking a little uncomfortable, gets up and starts to leave the meeting and me behind.

"I'll meet you at the car, Jayd. I have to make a call. Later," Jeremy says to the rest of the group. I hope everything's OK.

"Later, dude," Chance says. "Matt, I think you're on to something here. I've got the perfect song, too." We all agree that Chance and I will perform the old-school cut, *Can I Get A . . .* by Jay-Z for our campaign day next week and win some cool voting points for our clique. The topic of this song is just right to get me and Chance going. After all, it was our debate about guys exchanging cheddar for girls' cookies that inspired Matt's suggestion in the first place. Besides, the hook is contagious and will stay in people's minds long after the performance, which is just what we want.

"Rehearsals will start tomorrow during lunch and after school and continue everyday until we perform next week. Meeting adjourned." As we all scramble away from the drama room, I can't help but worry about Jeremy's reaction to me performing with Chance. I wonder what that's all about?

~ 9 ~

A Slice of Beef

"Bring beef to your house
Like a Chinese take out."

—ALKAHOLIKS

Even with Nellie's objection to being on stage at Wednesday's meeting, we still think it would be a good idea. I asked Nellie again yesterday before our first rehearsal at lunch, but she adamantly refused, saying she has stage fright. I think it would be a good idea for her to be a part of the performance, if for no other reason than to give her more visibility. We spent all of our time yesterday rehearsing or passing out pamphlets and pins with Nellie's face plastered all over them. Seth also set up a page for Nellie's campaign on the Drama Club's Web site. Nellie definitely has full exposure now, giving ASB and the athletes and cheerleaders something to worry about.

All of her newfound fame is making me worry too. As homecoming week approaches, I can't help but to keep recalling my dream about her and Chance getting blasted with paint guns. The more I think about it, the more I know it's some kind of warning. But, how do I change the future if I'm not exactly sure of her enemy's identity? With the Misty and KJ drama, it was so simple because my enemies were all up in my face. I just didn't heed my dreams in time to avoid most of the drama. But, this time is different.

I'm just glad it's Friday and I can escape all of this week's BS. I'm also glad Jeremy invited me to have an early dinner with him at his favorite pizza spot. Chance and Nellie came with us to discuss more campaign strategies. And, I've decided to go the session tonight with Raheem and Nigel, if for no other reason than to let off some steam.

"So, tell the truth. Did Michael steal his wife from Reid's older brother?" I ask as I dig into the hot pizza on the table in front of us. Pizza by the Slice is the only authentic New York–style pizza parlor around here. Jeremy and his brothers should own half the business as much as he claims they eat here.

"Where'd you hear that?" Jeremy says, getting a very serious face all of a sudden. Nellie and Chance look at each other and then back at me, waiting for my response.

"I didn't hear it anywhere," I say, putting the hot slice into my mouth and taking a bite before continuing. I actually didn't hear it anywhere. After talking to Ms. Toni about the whole family feud thing, I came up with my own reasoning, and, from his response, I don't think I'm too far off. "I'm just trying to figure out what could make y'all hate each other so much, since you won't give up all the family secrets," I say, brushing my shoulder up against his. Our quaint booth is a couple's dream, if that couple's getting along.

"You're putting a lot on this, Jayd," Jeremy says, looking slightly amused at my detective work. He takes a slice from the hot pie and folds it in half like a hot dog before biting into it. He's a pro at eating pizza.

"Christi and Ted used to date back in high school," Jeremy says, casually dropping some juicy information. Now, that's the root of all this beef. It's always over a girl and some dude's fragile ego being broken.

"What he's not telling you, Jayd, is that Christi and Michael almost died in a car accident on prom night. They can't prove it, but everybody knows Ted had something to do with it," Chance says, adding more sauce to the mix. Nellie looks even more interested in the full story than I am.

"So, what happened?" Nellie says, picking at her single slice of cheese pizza. Chance, Jeremy, and I are sharing a large pepperoni.

"What do you think happened?" Chance responds. "When Michael got out of the hospital, he promptly whipped Ted's ass. And, Justin and Jeremy got in a couple of kicks too," Chance says, giving his boy dap. Jeremy looks like none of this affects him anymore. But, it obviously does or he'd be taking me to the dance.

"Now, will you get off my back about not going to the dance with you?" Jeremy says. "Besides, even if I wanted too, my mom would never forgive me," he says.

"Why would your mom care?" I ask. "And, since when does your mom stop you from doing anything?"

"My mom believes my brothers and I should be loyal to one another," he says. A sense of pride has just claimed his head like a crown. "We do a lot of stupid shit together and separately. But, one thing remains. No matter what, we stand by one another. And, that includes not going to any more school functions as long as a Connelly is in charge."

"Hey, you and Chance should go together," Nellie offers, trying to bring a little lightness to the serious mood. But, the look on Jeremy's face doesn't agree.

"I don't mind taking my girl," Chance says, not aware of Jeremy's emotion. "What color are you wearing?" he asks.

"I don't have a dress yet," I answer. "But, I may already have a date," I say, trying to get out of this without much protest. I don't know why Jeremy looks the way he does. But, I know showing up with Chance isn't the right thing to do.

"Really?" Nellie asks. "Who?" she persists, trying to blow my cover.

"I'm not saying anything until it's solid," I say. I'll ask Nigel to be my homecoming escort tonight when he picks me up, since he doesn't seem interested in asking Nellie. And, I'm sure he's not bringing his steady girlfriend. Being the true player that he is, he knows better than to mix up his dual school identities. He'll keep his Westingle connection through her—whoever she is—and keep whatever profile he creates for himself at South Bay on the low.

"Whatever, Jayd. You know you ain't gotta date," Chance says, snatching up his third slice. "And what about you, Nellie? Who's the lucky dude?" Chance asks, rubbing up against Nellie's side with his arm.

"I don't have an escort yet," Nellie says, giving me the evil eye. I know she wants me to get Nigel to ask her. But, I ain't doing that to my girl. Knowing Nigel, he would happily oblige, taking advantage of Nellie and putting me in an impossible situation between two of my closest friends. I make it a habit of never willingly hooking my girls up with dogs, no matter how charming and cute they are.

"I think you two should go together," I say, gesturing to Chance and Nellie. "It makes sense," I say, not mentioning the fact Chance can offer Nellie the much needed protection my dream predicts she'll need.

"You're joking, right?" Nellie says. "I thought you said you were hooking me up with a friend of yours," she persists, about to intentionally blow my cover if I don't give in to her silent demand.

"I was, but he turned out to be taken," I say, not wanting to give up all my info. She needs to shut up about Nigel and now.

"Really? Because it didn't sound like that the other day," she continues, as relentless as a pit bull. Why can't she take a hint? "As a matter of fact, I could've sworn he was very interested," she says, getting hella salty. Maybe I should hook her up with Nigel and let him check her oversize ego. I can testify to the manipulative skills of Nigel and his friends.

"Nellie, can we talk about this later?" I say, feeling uncom-

fortable. Chance and Jeremy smile at each other while shaking their heads. I know what their thinking.

"Girls," Jeremy says admonishingly, while picking up the
empty pizza tray and returning it to the counter, where the
cashier promptly removes it. The few other customers in
the spot are hella young and playing video games, not interested in our conversation at all.

"Ladies, please," Chance says, getting up to join Jeremy
who's made his way to the door, indicating he's ready to
leave. Chance pulls out a pack of cigarettes and his Zippo
lighter, ready for a smoke break. Nellie and I are still seated
in the booth and looking hard at each other.

"Nellie, what the hell is your problem?" I ask, shocked
that, after all I've sacrificed for her this week she's acting like
a little brat. Or better yet, a spoiled princess.

"My problem is you can't have everything you want, Jayd.
You have to make some choices and give the rest of us a
chance," she says, seriously tripping. If she thinks I want
Nigel to myself, she's got another thing coming. Why do all
girls have to possess a little broad in them?

"Nellie, what the hell are you talking about?" I ask, ready
to check her in front of everyone.

"Yeah, Nellie, what, or rather, who are you talking about?"
Chance asks, looking from her to Jeremy, who, judging by
the look on his face was just thinking the same thing. I can
see why they're such good friends.

"I'm talking about Nigel," Nellie says, leaving no holds
barred. This girl's on one for real. It's a trip what jealousy will
do to a person. But, I don't need any more beef in my life right
now. So, I need to diffuse this situation and quick. Jeremy's looking real interested and I don't want him to get any more ideas.

"Nellie, like I said. I already asked him for you and he said
he's got a girlfriend," I say. But, she still doesn't look sympathetic.

"So he can go with you, but not with me," she says, seeing straight into my thoughts. "What's that all about?" Nellie asks, shocking me, Chance, and most of all Jeremy. He looks like he's just been betrayed and I could kill Nellie for stirring up more shit.

"We're friends from way back in the day," I say, trying to make it sound insignificant. "If we were to go, which we haven't even discussed yet, it wouldn't be a date, which it would be if you two went together." Looking a little less defensive, Nellie gets up and stands next to Chance, who's waiting for her next move.

"So, you know Nigel," Jeremy asks, walking over to give me a hand out of the booth. "Why am I just now finding out about this?" he asks.

"No reason. I just haven't had a chance to tell you about it, with all the homecoming stuff going on," I say, not wanting to lie about my association with Nigel any longer. But, I'm still not ready to tell him all about Raheem.

"So, how do you know Nigel?" Chance asks, diverting some of Jeremy's heat from me and leading the way out the restaurant and toward the parking lot.

"We went to junior high together," I say, holding on tight to Jeremy's hand. "I haven't seen or talked to him in years."

"Well, why you didn't just say that in the beginning? Never mind. I'm sure it's some chick thing and I don't want to know," Chance says, completely calming the situation and opening the passenger door for Nellie to get in. "Need a ride home, miss junior class homecoming princess to be?" he says, making Nellie smile and lighten up a bit. She can be so damn volatile sometimes.

"Yes, I do. And Jayd, I'm sorry I got so upset," Nellie says, making me question her sanity. She can switch up so fast. This homecoming shit has gone straight to her head and is leaving no room for straight thinking.

"No problem," I say, not wanting to chew her out in front of Jeremy and Chance. Some things are best left for private. But, she will get told for airing my laundry, especially over a dude she barely knows.

"Get her home safely," Jeremy says to Chance as he gets in his car and speeds off, leaving Jeremy and me to deal with our own issues.

"What was that look you gave about Chance taking me to the dance?" I ask as we head up Pacific Coast Highway toward Inglewood, our now customary Friday route to my mom's.

"It was nothing," he says, not even denying it. So, it must be something good.

"Enough with the secrets," I declare, tired of his tendency to avoid uncomfortable conversations. "If we're going to make it as a couple, you have to tell me the truth," I say, feeling the contradiction of my own words. Here I am sweating the clock because I have to get ready for the session tonight and I haven't even told him about the first one last weekend. I tell myself I'm just waiting for the right time. But truthfully, I'm afraid of Jeremy's reaction.

"Fine, Jayd," he says, finally giving in to me. "Chance used to have a crush on you," he says, not telling me anything new.

"So?" I say. "I used to have a crush on him too. It's no big deal," I say, making light of it. Our crushes didn't last long and we've been friends ever since.

"Well, then you can see why I might be a little concerned with the two of you going to a dance together," he says. I never realized how jealous Jeremy really is. Ms. Toni was right. These Weiner boys can be possessive when they feel threatened.

"Now I know you're not worried about me and Chance," I say, taking my hand from its customary position on his thigh and crossing my arms over my chest. "Before you, I wasn't really into White guys, Chance included," I say, trying to reassure him of how special our relationship is. "You apparently are used to interracial dating. This is a first for me and I don't take it lightly. Chance knows this about us and, because he's my friend, would never do anything to jeopardize our relationship," I say, hoping my words are sinking in.

"Yeah, I know Chance is a good guy. But, you hide shit too, Jayd. Like this whole Nigel thing. What's up with that?" he asks, speeding into the twist and turns of the highway, ignoring the congested traffic. His music is blaring, making it difficult to communicate.

"OK, baby. It's time I came clean about something else too," I say, setting him up for my news. "I went out last Friday with Nigel and another old friend from junior high," I say, easing my way into a confession.

"That's not a big deal, Jayd," Jeremy says. "What's a big deal is you keeping it from me," he says. "Are we going to have a relationship based on trust or secrets?" Jeremy asks. I wish I could rewind time to our first kiss and stay there forever. Every time I get into a relationship, there's more drama. That's why dating, as opposed to being in a committed relationship, isn't such a bad state to be in. Because, when the titles come, the feelings of ownership and entitlement also begin.

"I'm sorry I kept it from you," I say. "No more secrets, I promise." But, can I really say that? I can't tell Jeremy everything. That wouldn't be smart. I just have to do a better job at not getting into situations that require me to keep things from my man if I want this relationship to work.

After twenty minutes of riding in silence, Jeremy pulls up to my mom's house and parks. We sit for a few minutes more, listening to the music without saying a word. Finally, Jeremy unbuckles his seat belt, leans over to me and kisses my lips, making me forget all about our issues.

~ 10 ~
Solo

*"I can feel this for sure/
I've been here before."*

—TEENA MARIE

When Nigel picks me up, it's already past ten. Jeremy and I took our time getting out of the car this evening making up, which didn't give me but an hour to get ready. So, instead of my usual cornrows, I washed my hair and left the conditioner in, pulling my soft waves back into a tight bun at the base of my neck. Wearing my mom's big, gold bamboo hoops, I hope to draw attention away from my large forehead.

"What's up, baby girl?" Nigel says, pulling into the long driveway, alongside my mother's apartment building.

"What's up, Nigel?" I say, squeezing in between the car door and brick wall, not wanting to scratch up the classic Impala.

"Damn, baby, be careful," he says, more concerned about the door than me.

"Shut up Nigel," I say, narrowly making it into my seat. We back out of the driveway and head toward Raheem's' house with the music up loud enough for everyone to hear. It feels good being out. I miss the exhilaration of going to the studio late at night. It's just something about being around good music and peaceful vibes that makes it worth all the drama.

"So, what's up with your White boy? Did you tell him I'm

your baby daddy yet?" he says, making light of my looming dilemma.

"Yes, I told him about us knowing each other from back in the day. But, that's all he knows." I still didn't have the heart to tell Jeremy about tonight's session or the fact my now friend is my former first love. Why is shit so difficult sometimes? Well, I'm just glad I'm not in my mom's position with Ras Joe. Their breakup isn't going well at all. He's damn near stalking her and I think his woman knows about my mom too. She's been real secretive about the whole thing. But, I get little insights from overheard cell conversations here and there.

"Damn, Jayd. What's the big deal? So, he finds out you and Raheem used to date. What's he going to do? Forbid you from hanging out with us?" he asks, not feeling the least bit threatened.

"No one can forbid me from doing anything, except Mama," I say. But, I don't think Jeremy would like me spending so much time with my ex. I would be hella pissed if I found out he was kicking it with Tania, no matter the circumstances. So, I can't front. If he asks me not to hang with Nigel and Raheem, I'd have to give it some serious thought.

"Now that's my Jayd," Nigel says. "I started to think you were becoming a little punk for this fool," he says, cruising down the crowded avenue.

"I'm not anyone's punk. At least not anymore," I say remembering the stupid shit I did in the name of love for Raheem. "But, I will respect my man's wishes," I say, making Nigel take his eyes off the road and look at me, not believing what he's hearing, I guess.

"Are you on crack or something?" Nigel says, heading up the hill only moments away from Raheem's house. "You better not ever sell us out for no White dude, Jayd. We go way, way back and that supersedes any dudes or females, for that matter." Nigel was always the most ride or die out of us all. Our crew was tight, though. If one of us had a fight with someone on the outside, we all did.

"Ain't nobody selling nobody out. Damn, you sound like them fools at school," I say. Even though I know he means well, unlike the folks at school, he does remind me of Shae, and that ain't cool at all. Sensing my disappointment, Nigel takes one hand of the steering wheel and places it on top of mine. When we reach Raheem's, he parks in the driveway, turns off the engine, and talks to me.

"All I'm saying is that he ain't the one, Jayd. Now, you can go and have your little fun with him or whatever. And, if he's that serious to you, then bring him to a session one night. That's how much we love you, girl. But, we all know he's temporary. Your real man is inside," Nigel says. Before I can protest, Kamal runs up to the car, opening my door.

"Jayd!" he screams, practically pulling me to my feet. At eight years old, the boy's almost as tall as I am, making me remember how I got the nickname Lyttle in the first place.

"Kamal, be careful, boy. She's precious cargo," Raheem says, following him to the driveway.

"Hey, Rah," I say, looking at him over Kamal's shoulder. After letting me out of the tight embrace, Kamal runs back up the driveway toward the house.

"Rah took me to Shakey's," Kamal says. "Want some chicken and Mojo potatoes?" he asks from the porch.

"No, thank you, lil man. I just ate," I say, laughing at his enthusiasm. It must be nice to be so young and innocent. I wish I could just be happy with some food.

"Well, I didn't," Nigel says, following Kamal into the house. "I'll catch up with y'all in a minute," he says, leaving me alone with Raheem.

"So, do I get a hug?" Rah says, pulling me into his arms without waiting for a reply. His hugs are entrancing, reminding me of long afternoons spent behind the bleachers, hiding from the rest of the world. I've always felt so safe in his arms.

"How was your week?" I ask as we head into the house, ready to start the session.

"It was cool," he says, passing up Kamal and Nigel and leading me through the kitchen to the studio. I still can't get over how much work he's done in here. When Rah sets his mind to something he wants, there's no stopping him. "I got an A on my history paper. That was the toughest shit I've ever been through. But, it was worth it. And, you?"

"My week was OK," I say as Nigel comes in, interrupting our twosome.

"Hey, Rah. Did Jayd tell you she's keeping you a secret from her man?"

"Nigel," I say, smacking him in the head. Why is he such a hater? "That's not any of his business."

"Oh, so now you're keeping secrets from me too," Rah says, teasing me. "You're not the honest and upright Jayd Jackson I once knew and loved," he says revealing his perfectly straight teeth. When did he get his braces removed?

"I'm not keeping secrets," I say, defending my logic. "I'm just waiting for the right time to ask him to a session," I say, calling Nigel's earlier bluff.

"We don't allow just anyone to the sessions, Jayd. You know that," Raheem says, becoming territorial over his precious studio. Unlike other artists, Nigel and Raheem keep the energy in their space completely professional.

"Nigel said I could invite him one night. Besides, I think it's time y'all go to know each other, since we're friends and he's my man, right?" I say. Nigel's sitting back, enjoying the show, or so I think.

"Jayd, you're full of shit, you know that?" Nigel says, stuffing the last of his Mojo potatoes from a napkin into his mouth.

"What are you talking about?" I ask, defensively. "You just

told me if Jeremy means that much to me then I should invite him over," I say, repeating his words for Rah to hear, who
doesn't look amused.

"Yeah, if he's the one for you," he says, giving Raheem a
nod and walking over to the booth, ready for work. "Which
he ain't and you're the only one still in denial about that."
With that, Nigel goes into the soundproof booth, closing the
door shut behind him. Rah looks at me, reading my thoughts
without saying a word. We both know this road all too well. I
plop down onto the couch, watching Raheem set up the beat
for Nigel's flow.

Raheem and I will always be more than friends. It's a fact
that no matter who he's dating or who I'm dating, there's always room for us. We don't have to touch to feel our connection. And, after seeing Jeremy's true jealous personality, I
know he's not going to understand our relationship. Maybe
this is what Mama meant by telling me to talk to my mother
about making half assed decisions. I really just want the answer to one question: Will I ever be happy with a man?

I have always secretly envied my mom's skin. Her perfectly smooth ebony complexion matches Nellie's perfectly.
Sometimes I think they should be mother and daughter. I've
always admired the fact that their complexion hides blem-
ishes flawlessly, looks better in bright colors, and seems to
have a timeless royalty about it.

"Hey, baby. How was work?" she says, stretching like a
Siamese cat across her sofa, reminding me of how nice a nap
would be in the middle of the afternoon. I only have a few
hours before I have to get ready for my date with Jeremy
tonight and I'm exhausted from last night's session. I also
need to get started on Mama's assignment.

"It was cool. How was home?" I say, laughing at her. She

works hard all week in an office, so she deserves to chill on the weekend.

"Actually, your aunt Vivica and I went to Robinson's May. You know they've closed just about all of them now," she says, sounding really sad about it.

"Yeah, so I heard. Did you buy anything nice fore me?" I ask, already knowing the answer to that question.

"No, but I bought plenty of stuff for you to borrow," she says, getting up from her spot and walking toward the kitchen. "And I talked to Mama this morning," she says. "What's this I hear about you choosing my path?" Her path? I don't remember Mama mentioning my mother writing down her story in the book. According to Mama, a path is only valid if it's been recorded.

"What are you talking about?" I say, following her into the kitchen and taking a sip out of her cup. Bailey's and Cream. I lucked out.

"Jayd," she says, snatching the cup from my hand and giving me an evil look. "I'm serious. Mama's pissed at you for not studying your lessons. She wants you to take your legacy seriously, unlike me and your auntie," she says, putting the cup down and leaning up against the counter, watching me leave the crowded kitchen and head into the bathroom.

"But, why me? Why now?" I say, feeling a little overwhelmed. I come here to get away from Mama's house. I know she reigns supreme no matter where I go. But still, with my mom breathing down my neck about my spirit work, I feel like Mama's here. I can't get any time off.

"I don't know why, Jayd. But, Mama's always felt you were special. She says that's why I hooked up with your crazy ass Daddy in the first place, to get your exceptional behind here. So, study your lessons and keep Mama off both our backs," she says, slamming the refrigerator door shut after taking out half its contents and placing the food on the kitchen counter. I hope she cooks. That would be a nice treat.

"But, how did you get a choice?" I yell as I change out of my work clothes and into some basketball shorts, a sports bra, and a clean head rag, ready for a good nap.

"Mama was too busy having babies to really worry about me. And, at that time, she was very busy in the church with Daddy. So, I never saw any of Mama's spiritual side until I was in high school. By then, she and Daddy were at war."

"Well, that battle's still going on," I say, walking back into the kitchen and retrieving a skillet from the top cabinet to fry the ground turkey. My mom can cook three things very well: lasagna, lemon meringue pie, and tacos, which is my favorite and tonight's choice. Even though she's going through some BS with Ras Joe, I'm still glad she's home for a change. It's nice when we have time to cook together.

"Girl, you had better catch up in your reading. This is about the age Mama will give up on you. She's not known for her patience, ya know," my mom says, shaking the package of Lawry's Taco seasoning before adding it to the water, pouring it in my skillet full of browning meat.

"I know, I know," I say, feeling guilty enough already. If Mama talked to my mom about it, I know she's really hurt. They usually only talk about the mundane stuff that keeps a relationship going. So, this must be serious.

"And, what were you thinking not finishing Maman Marie's story?" she asks, taking the corn tortillas out of the package and putting them in the hot cast-iron skillet full of olive oil. She puts just a pinch of salt in the skillet before individually placing each tortilla in, submerging them completely. It smells like a Mexican restaurant in here. My mom takes a sip of her drink and continues to gently grind me. "How could you put it down?" she says, now chopping up the lettuce and tomatoes. She passes the cheese grater and a big block of sharp cheddar cheese to me.

"I actually was very interested, but I just haven't had time to become completely engrossed in it. But so far, I see a lot of the similarities between her love life and ours. Why don't you spring for pregrated cheese?" I ask. This is always my job and I hate doing it. It reminds me of Mama making me grate cocoa butter, shea butter, black soap, and any other thing that needs grating in her spirit room.

"Grating that cheese is the least of your problems, Jayd," she says, stirring the simmering taco meat and turning the heat off. She carefully takes the golden tortillas out of the skillet and lays them on the flattened paper bag to absorb the grease. "Mama thinks you've got it," she says, transferring the tortillas to a paper plate and passing them to me. I put the plate on the dining room table and walk back into the crammed kitchen to get the taco sauce, Red Rooster, and two cans of Coke out of the refrigerator.

"Got what?" I say, already knowing the answer to my question. I've had to hear the story of my unusual birth all of my life. And, I've also had to hear about how my caul, or my veil of sight, wasn't properly cared-for according to Mama, which set my destiny off on a difficult path. And, how my eyes aren't green like Mama's, my Mom's and Maman Marie's, leading Mama to doubt if I actually inherited the Williams women sight.

"Girl, don't play silly with me. Mama told me about your dreams, Jayd. And, interpreting dreams is a big part of having the sight," she says. "I didn't take any of my visions or my spirit work seriously. And now, the sight doesn't come to me anymore," she says, sounding sad again.

"I know it's a lot of work, Jayd," my mom says, taking a seat at the dining table. I love her tacos and I sit ready to throw down too. "But I honestly think you're up to the task," she says, digging into the taco meat and condiments. Instead of folding our tacos, we break the shells into small pieces and scoop up the filling, Ethiopian style. I don't know why we eat our tacos like this, but we always have.

"I tried to explain to her I'm going through a lot at school right now and it's taking up most of my time," I say. I didn't realize how tired and sore I was, but now that I've worked a full day today after being out all night, I feel it. After rehearsing Thursday and Friday and running around like a mad woman publicizing Nellie, I'm really whipped.

"That's what I meant by following my path. I never wanted to be different. I just wanted to chill with my girls, live a good life and have some peace. Living with Mama was never peaceful," my mom says, picking up her Coke and taking a sip while looking like she's about to drop some knowledge. "I just never wanted to know like you do, Jayd."

"But, that's just it, Mom. I don't know if I want to know right now," I say, scooping up the last of the taco mix on my plate, ready for more. "It's a lot to deal with and try to have a normal teenage life."

"Look, Jayd, if it's one thing I learned from being one of Mama's daughters it's that your life will never settle down," she says, also going for seconds. "And, had I taken advantage of Mama's spiritual legacy, I would know how to deal with this bull out here in the real world."

"So, what you're saying is I should choose to study my spirit work so I can better handle high school, but at the same time sacrifice my social life? That doesn't seem fair," I say, not meaning to sound like a baby. But, damn, I want the best of both worlds.

"It's time to grow up, Jayd. You're going to have to make a decision about which path you want to walk, and soon. This is all leading up to the first leg of your initiation into womanhood, Jayd. And, Mama ain't gone wait for long to test you. You think all your little quizzes and assignments are something. Wait until Mama really tests you. Then you'll know for sure whether or not you're the one."

"Which one?" I say. I feel like I'm in the ghetto version of *The Matrix* or something.

"The one to break the cycle of screwed up relationships that divert us from our true legacy of fierce warrior womanhood," she says, clearing the table. "One of Mama's favorite heroes is Queen Califia, Queen of California, a.k.a. 'the land where Black women live,'" my mom says, without as much as a blink. Is she serious? "Queen Califia is the namesake for our Golden State. Have you gotten that far in your history lessons yet?" she asks, referring to Mama's secret recipe book.

"No, I haven't and I've never heard of California having a queen," I say.

"Yeah, there's a picture of her in the book. The point is she has a legacy just like we all do. Read about your ancestors and other heroes and consciously choose who you want to emulate," my mom says, returning to her spot on the couch, ready for another nap. I now have less than two hours before my date and I feel heavier than ever, another trait in my blood. Well, I wonder if Jeremy can handle all the woman I apparently am going to be.

~ 11 ~
Visible Evidence

*"If you must dance,
Dance for me."*

—ME'SHELL NDEGEOCELLO

When Jeremy gets here, he finally comes in to meet my mom. Wearing some simple blue Levis, a Cal Berkeley T-shirt and his usual sandals, he looks adorable. His Irish Spring fresh scent precedes him into the apartment. I've also chosen a comfy pair of Levis and an orange V-neck T-shirt to wear with my gold sandals from our first shopping trip for tonight's date. My hair is still in a bun with the big earrings and gold bangle to match. I have to admit, we look pretty good from the outside. But, it's the core of our relationship I'm concerned with.

"This must be Jeremy," my mom says, greeting him at the door. "I was starting to think you didn't exist," she says, ushering him inside and winking at me over her shoulder.

"Well, I do," he says, seemingly flattered by my mother's flirting. "And, I see where Jayd gets her good looks from," he says, making my mother smile as she takes a seat next to him on the couch. I close the front door and walk over to the dining room to grab a seat for myself and watch my mom work her magic.

"So, where are you two lovebirds off to?" she asks, slightly embarrassing me.

"We're just going to hang with some friends by the beach,"

Jeremy says, referring to Matt's house. They're throwing a party for all of the homecoming nominees. I haven't talked to Nellie since yesterday's salty episode. But, I know she's going to be there. "Speaking of which, Jayd," he says. "Chance told me he convinced Nellie to go to the dance with him." First Misty's wishes come true, now Chance's. The miracles just keep on coming, don't they?

"Well, I guess there goes another backup date for me," I say, making light of the fact that I still don't have a date to the dance. I'm afraid to ask Nigel because of what Nellie may think. As stupid as she can act sometimes, she's still my girl and I don't want her to feel like I'm keeping her from getting to know Nigel.

"Why would you need a backup when you have all this man sitting right here to take you?" my mom says, putting us both on the spot. I forgot to mention Jeremy's not taking me to homecoming or any other dance for that matter. I know she won't get it at all. She was a queen, princess, or runner-up for every dance at Compton High back in her day. And, like most royalty, she considers it an honor to be an escort.

"She needs a date because unfortunately, I can't take her," Jeremy says, breaking the news to my mom, whose face expresses her full shock and disappointment. She loves the whole scene: getting dressed, taking pictures, all of it. I knew she would have a problem with me not having a date. For her, a girl going stag to a dance isn't even a consideration.

"Oh, do you have to work or something?" my mom asks, totally confused. "What kind of boss won't give you the day off for your homecoming?" she asks, looking from me to him in disbelief.

"The kind that gives birth to you," he says, referring to his mother.

"You can't take my daughter to homecoming because your mother won't let you?" my mom says, getting up like she's been personally insulted. "Does she have a problem with you going to the dance with Jayd because she's Black?" my mom asks, taking our conversation to a whole other level.

"No, no. Not at all," Jeremy says, getting up to both defend himself and reassure my mother, who's not hearing a word of what he's saying. "My mom loves Jayd." Well, I don't know about all that. But, judging by her sons' preferences in women, I think she's over the whole interracial dating thing.

"Mom, it's not about me. It's about his brother and a whole bunch of other stuff we can't get into right now. But, it's not about me being Black. I promise," I say, calming her down. She looks like she's about to get out her afro pick and whip Jeremy's ass with it.

"OK, whatever," my mom says, ready to settle in for the night and watch reruns of *Charmed*, one of our favorite shows. "I guess Jayd will fill me in later, although I still won't understand why you, as my daughter's boyfriend, can't take her to the first dance of the year," she says, looking at me like I've been holding out on her about Jeremy, which I have. "And, I'm sorry about jumping on you," she says.

"It's all good. Jayd's like that sometimes too," he says before giving my mother a hug and walking toward the door.

"Shut up, Jeremy," I say, getting up from my seat and kissing my mother good night before following Jeremy out.

"It was nice meeting you, Ms. Jackson," he says, assuming my mother and I have the same last name. But, she promptly went back to her maiden name after she and my father divorced and is always quick to correct the mistake.

"It's James. But, you can call me Lynn," she says. She hates when my friends call her Ms. James. She says it makes her feel like an old woman, which by anyone's standards, my mom is definitely not.

"All right, Lynn. I'll have your daughter home at a decent

time," he says, smiling. He seems pleasantly surprised with his first encounter with my mom.

"Have fun chillaxing," I say. "And, don't open the door without asking who it is first," I add, only half joking. My mom's had trouble with dudes before, but she's a little more worried than usual about Ras Joe.

"Be careful with my baby. She's got a lot of work to do," my mom says, reminding me of my duties. Can a sistah get a break?

"I will," Jeremy says, taking my hand as we step down the stairs and walk toward his Mustang parked at the end of the driveway. Seeing his clean, classic car still gives me goose bumps.

"Your mom seems more like your sister," he says, opening the door for me. "She doesn't look like she's had any kids at all." My mom works extra hard to keep her petite body in shape. She hits the gym every day after work and walks on the weekend.

"Haven't you heard, baby?" I say as he gets in the driver's seat, choosing tonight's theme music. Depeche Mode. Now, that's old-school alternative. Bryan and Tarek both play some of this on their shows. Otherwise, I wouldn't be hip.

"Heard what?" he says, backing out and heading toward Redondo Beach. It's a cool night and the air feels good on my face. Finally, winter is coming. Well, as much of a winter as we get in LA.

"Black don't crack," I say, making him chuckle a little. I'm glad he met my mom and they liked each other. Well, except when she thought his mother was the Grand Wizard of the KKK.

"Yeah, but apparently, it doesn't get fat, either. If that's how you'll look after having a baby, sign me up to be the daddy," he says, tickling my stomach. What's gotten in to him tonight? He's in an unusually playful mood.

"Watch the road, man. Watch the road," I say, returning his hand to the steering wheel. I hope he's still playful when I ask him where our relationship is headed. I need to know just how serious Jeremy is about me before I tell him about Raheem.

When we arrive at Matt's house, the party's in full effect with people hangin' outside, in the entryway and generally all over the house. Everyone affiliated with the Drama Club is here and having a ball from the sound of it. That's when I notice Tania and her rich girls' clique hangin' out on the front porch, looking hella faded. We can't help but pass them as we enter through the front.

"Oh, look, isn't it South Bay's newest couple," Tania says, slurring a little. I've never seen her at a social function. So, I don't know how she really gets down. But, by the smell of it, I'd say straight tequila.

"What's up, Tania," Jeremy says, leading me past the sad scene and through the foyer to the kitchen. I saw Chance's Nova parked in the driveway, so I assume Nellie's here with him. I guess she got over her fear of being seen in an old car around her hood.

"Jeremy, what did you ever see in her?" I ask, not really caring about his answer. I just want him to know how lucky he is to be with me and that I know it.

"Sex," he says, stepping through the back kitchen door and down the flight of stairs leading into the basement. As usual, the lights are very dim and the smoke, thick. When my eyes adjust to the light, I see familiar faces playing pool, drinking, and lounging around the shiny cars on display.

"For real?" I say, not knowing how to respond to his candor. He really caught me off guard with that one. Now, every time I see Tania's face, I'll think of them doing it, even if he's just joking.

"Yes, for real. Sometimes it's just physical, Jayd. You mean to tell me you've never had a solely physical relationship with a guy?" he asks, sitting down on the same plush couch we sat on last time we were here, minus Nellie and Chance. Where are they, I wonder?

"Jeremy, I haven't had a physical relationship with anyone," I say, sitting next to him on the couch and looking around for Nellie. Maybe she's outside by the pool.

"OK, Lady J. You can play the innocent act all you want. But, I know you've had a sexual relationship with someone," he says, not knowing anything at all about my sex life, or lack there of.

"Jeremy, I'm a virgin," I say. For the first time I think I've fully shocked him. Although Raheem and I have tested the limits of what virginity actually is and, KJ to some extent also, I've never gone all the way.

"You mean to tell me you've never had sex, ever?" he says, the most interested I've seen him in me all night. Just as it's getting good, Chance and Nellie come in from outside.

"What's up with ya," Chance says, reaching down to give Jeremy dap and me a hug. Nellie, right behind him, takes a seat in one of the two chairs across from us before saying her hellos.

"So, how's your night going so far?" Nellie says, making small talk. I can tell she's still a little irritated with me from yesterday. But, she needs to get over herself.

"Just fine," I answer, wishing she'd stop being so catty. "I hear you and Chance are going to the dance together," I say, a tad bitter. She could have told me herself instead of letting me hear it through the grapevine.

"Yeah, I think it's a good idea to show up with a member of my sponsoring group," she says, sounding all official about it. But, Chance couldn't care less. He looks like he's on cloud nine.

"Yeah, but you know what they say. Your date for homecoming will be your date for the prom," Chance says, remaining ever hopeful and setting up our topic of discussion for this evening. But, before we can get started, Matt comes over and offers us all drinks.

"Well if it isn't the debating thespians," he says, mocking our tendency to have serious conversations.

"Some people enjoy a healthy debate," I say, ready for who ever wants a piece of me tonight. I've had it with dudes and their wants and desires. Sometimes it has to be about what girls need too.

"And some people want to relax and enjoy the view," Jeremy says, ready for round one. "That's what's wrong with society. We put too much pressure on every situation, making it more than it's meant to be," he says, accepting one of the Guinnesses Matt offers us.

"I agree," Nellie adds. "Take, for example, this dance. It doesn't matter who you end up going with. It doesn't have to predict who you'll end up with by the end of the year," she says, glancing in Chance's direction. I hope he's smart enough to understand she's just using him.

"Yeah, but it's still a very important social event," Matt says, leaning up against Nellie's chair. "Who you go with says a lot about what you want people to think of your relationship with the other person," he says, pleading my case to Jeremy without me saying a word. I can feel Jeremy tense up next to me, dreading where this conversation's headed. Right on cue, Misty, KJ, Shae, and Tony walk in, drawing our attention away from the topic at hand. What the hell are they doing here?

"What's up, KJ?" Matt says in KJ's direction as he leads his entourage straight for us. Matt's a huge basketball fan. I'm sure he'd never thought he'd see the day KJ was at his house.

"What are you drinking?" Matt says, pointing to the full bar with a bar attendant ready to serve.

"Nothing right now, man. But thanks," KJ says, smiling at me.

"Hey, Jayd. Now I can see why you sold out to be around these White folks. They got it going on out here," Shae says, giving her crew a chuckle at my expense.

"Whatever. What are y'all doing here?" I ask impatiently.

"We came to support South Bay High's first Black princess nominee," Misty says, sounding patriotic. When did she become a cheerleader for Nellie? And, more importantly, when did KJ start hanging out with Misty at night? What the hell?

"What's up with y'all?" Nellie asks, basically inviting them to sit with us. Has she lost her damned mind? Has she forgotten these are my enemies? And, most of all that Jeremy and KJ tried to kill each other the last time they were together? She's really on a trip with this whole princess shit and it's getting on my nerves.

"Uhmm, Jayd, we need to get some air," Chance says, sensing the vibe tensing up. Jeremy gets up with him and I decide to go too.

"Don't leave on my account," KJ says to me as I follow Jeremy outside.

"Oh, don't worry. I am," I say, giving him the evil eye before shooting a look at Nellie, who just looks like she was waiting for me to go. I hope she doesn't think she's about to take over my Drama friends because she's one of their nominees. I'm trying to tell her these White folks up here are cool, but they ain't that cool. But, it looks like she's just going to have to fall on her own.

After leaving Chance at the bong house, Jeremy and I decide to leave and continue our evening at our favorite spot:

the beach, which is the perfect place for us to talk more seriously about our relationship. Finally working up the guts, I decide to ask Jeremy the question that's been on my mind all night.

"Do you think we match?" I ask as we walk barefoot on the cold sand. I'm a little afraid of his answer. I think we make a cute couple and the attraction is definitely there. But, it seems we're just too different on a basic level.

"Why would you ask me that?" Jeremy replies.

"Well, it just seems this entire homecoming dance has put a strain on our relationship and I just want to know if you think I'm still a good match for you. Look, things have been real tense with us this evening and we haven't really had a chance to vibe," I say, hoping to ease at least a little of the tension between us. "Do you realize you haven't given me a kiss all night?"

"Jayd, I think you are the perfect match for me," he says, stopping our slow stride and pulling me into him. He kisses my forehead, my nose and then sucks on my neck like a gentle vampire. It feels so good I forget all about whatever issues we may have. I just want to stay in his arms for as long as I can.

When we get back to the car after what seems like hours of making out, he whips out a package from the backseat.

"Just because you won't have a date doesn't mean you shouldn't be the best-dressed girl there." The box has the logo of the store in the Marina with my red dream dress.

"Oh, Jeremy," I say, opening the box to reveal the silky gown. "I don't know what to say."

"How about you forgive me," he says, tilting my head toward his, kissing me. "I'm really sorry things are off to a bad start with this whole dance and all. But, that's just how my family is. I hope you understand and don't get scared off," he says, kissing me between each word.

"OK. But, only if you forgive me too," I say, opening the small visor mirror to catch the reflection of the bright fabric against my skin. Who am I to judge someone's family? Wait until he finds out about mine. Admiring my reflection, I notice several small marks on my neck. Oh, hell no he didn't.

"Jeremy, look what you did," I say, forgetting all about the dress as visions of Mama's hand across my face play in my head. She's going to kill me when she sees these marks all over my neck. She already thinks I'm too distracted by the boys in my life. Now there's physical proof that I've been spending too much time with Jeremy, or at least I know that's how she'll see it.

"Damn, baby. You bruise easily," he says, sounding as surprised as me by the hickeys on my neck. "Well, at least you can hide them with a scarf or something," he says, smiling like he's just marked his territory. I know that look. The first time I got a hickey was from Raheem and it wasn't on my neck. We were smart enough not to leave evidence where parents could see, like on my thighs or his chest, while still letting others know this person was taken.

"Jeremy, you can't go marking me up like a cat pissing on a couch," I say, flattered and vexed all at once.

"I'm sorry. I really didn't think I'd mark you up," he says, placing my dress back in the backseat before starting the car. "But, a little makeup should work." I hope he's right. Maybe my mom will have some sympathy on me and help me blend together some foundation to hide them from Mama before I get home tomorrow night.

~ 12 ~
Whose House

"Can ya can ya can ya bounce wit me, bounce wit me."

—JAY-Z

When I get home from work this afternoon, my mom helps me hide my hickeys with some bomb foundation from Clinique. I can't see a thing and hopefully neither will anyone else. I also do my hair before we leave. Since she isn't in a rush for a date or anything, I get to stay a little later than usual, which is always a relief.

"Don't forget to pack your foundation, Jayd," my mom says from her bedroom. "It's sitting in here on my dresser." I rise from my spot on the couch to go to her room and retrieve the makeup.

I would give anything for my own room, especially if I could decorate it. My mom has good taste. Her room is spacious enough to fit her queen-size bed and oak frame, two nightstands, and a dresser drawer with a vanity attached comfortably. She has mirrors on the back of her closet doors, saving her some space.

"Thanks for helping me with this," I say as I pick up the small bottle of brown liquid. We had to blend a few different shades to get it to look right.

"Not a problem, girl. Just be careful with those boys, Jayd. If I learned anything from the little bit of history in Mama's spirit book I did read, it's that men can get you into a whole lot of bull. Our stories aren't the fairy tales you see in the movies, but they're just as fascinating and filled with lessons like any you see in the video store. I always preferred reading about Mama's sheroes, as she calls them, than reading my lessons or the prayers," my mom says, sitting up on the edge of her bed and slipping on her sandals.

"I know. I have to finish reading Maman's story when I get home. And, I won't be getting anymore hickeys, I promise."

"I hope not. Coming home with marks all over your body is the quickest way to get on Mama's bad side for a long, long time. That's why I had to get out of her house as quick as possible. Between the hickeys and the tattoos, my days on earth were numbered as far as Mama was concerned." I can only imagine my mom living in the house with all of her brothers and Mama and Daddy. Looking at her now, I can't imagine her living with anyone else, which still makes me wonder why she would allow her only daughter to grow up under the same conditions. But, questioning my path doesn't change it so, back to Mama's house I go.

After picking out my clothes for tomorrow and catching up with Mama, I decide to come out to Mama's spirit room and catch up on my studying. Our conversation was a bit icy this evening, so I know she's still pissed at me. Besides, I really want to finish Maman Marie's story and learn more about Mama's sheroes, too. But, Maman is my top priority right now. I can't be out here all night.

It's always quiet back here, even when there's a bunch of drama going on in the main house. And, with Lexi guarding the door whenever someone's in here, no drama is allowed back here at any time.

"Maman Marie. Have you heard this story before?" I ask Lexi as she makes herself comfortable across the threshold. It must be nice to be a dog. She looks up at me and gives a nod as if to say "Of course, I have. Haven't you?"

"Oh, hush. I get enough heat from Mama. I don't need you sweating me too." Ignoring me completely, she falls off into her own dreams.

Sitting on the wooden stool, I put the heavy book on the worktable and turn to the chapter on Maman. Now, where was I? It's such a long story, with sketches of her and Jon Paul on most of the pages. Some sketches are of them smiling, some yelling, some with just one or the other and some incomplete. I wonder who the artist is?

One sketch in particular catches my attention. It's a picture of Jon choking Maman. And, on the next page a large woman appears over their heads, stopping Jon from killing Maman. The woman has a head wrap on, like the ones Mama wears when she's working. After reading further into Maman's history, I learn the spirit in the picture with Jon is Marie La Veau, Maman's namesake and a famous voodoo queen in New Orleans. If a woman has problems with a lover, she can call on the queen to help her in her time of need.

"Jayd," Mama said, "it's too late for you to be out there by yourself," Jay yells from the back door. Tomorrow's Monday and I need to get some sleep for the long week ahead of me. I guess I'll have to finish Maman's story another time. But, at least I got something out of her story. When the road gets too hard to walk alone, call on spiritual help to see you through. That's what I'll need to do to survive homecoming week. It's here and I'm not ready for any of the drama with Nellie, Raheem or Jeremy. But, I'll have to be if I want to make it though and be victorious, no matter how hard Nellie's tripping.

When I get to school this morning, the entire campus is dripping with red-and-white streamers. There are signs everywhere announcing the homecoming activities planned for the week. There are also signs with all the homecoming nominees plastered everywhere, including Nellie, and for the pep rally today, officially kicking off homecoming week.

"That bitch is on one," Mickey says, referring to our friend with the swollen ego. Nellie's been getting on her nerves all weekend too. And, Mickey's patience wears out much quicker than mine. So, I know she's at her peak.

"I know what you mean," I say. She's been rubbing me the wrong way too and enough's enough. She needs to be checked and I'm going to do it.

"I couldn't even stand to go to the party with her on Saturday because she pissed me off at the mall earlier, not like I really wanted to be around all those White folks on the weekend anyway," Mickey says, continuing to vent. As we walk toward the football field, with the rest of the pep rally crowd, I see Nigel and wave for him to come over. He should be with the rest of the football team who's probably already on the field.

"Why, what happened at the mall?" I ask Mickey. I'd rather her get her tirade out before my boy gets over here. No sense in everyone knowing our business.

"She tried on damn near every dress in Betsey Johnson and then had the nerve not to buy a single one," Mickey says. Mickey gets very emotional, especially when it comes to some of Nellie's selfish behavior.

"Well, why you didn't just leave her there? Lord knows you've done it enough times before," I say, telling the truth.

"I did. That's why she's avoiding me this morning. I think she called Chance to come and get her ass from Beverly Hills. She needs to get a license or a bus pass, because I'm done being her damn driver," Mickey says, finishing her story just as Nigel gets here.

"Hey, Jayd, Mickey," he says, shining his biggest player smile at my girl. He's really feeling her. And, from the looks of it, Mickey likes the attention.

"What's up, Nigel," Mickey says, giving him a hug. Since when are they hugging? I asked her to pump information from him. But, I didn't know they were friends now.

"Is there something I need to know?" I say to them as they're still locked in each other's arms. What the hell? I wonder if Nellie knows Mickey's her actual threat and not me. Oh, this is going to be some shit.

"Mickey, what are you thinking?" I say, pulling her away from Nigel, who's just grinning. "What are you laughing at?" I say, pushing him as we continue toward the rally.

"You, trying to play like we all ain't got a little something on the side," he says, putting himself between me and Mickey as we walk down the steep hill toward the bottom bleachers as the rest of the lunch crowd settles in around us. This is when I can see just how big and White the student population really is.

"We all don't. And, don't get me all twisted up in whatever mess y'all stirring up. I don't want to know nothing," I say, serious as a heart attack. I have enough problems without managing one of Mickey's illustrious affairs. That's usually Nellie's department even though she hates doing it. But, I guess I've moved up the home girl notch for Mickey until Nellie comes back to her senses.

"Well, that's going to be kind of hard to do since I invited Mickey to the studio Saturday," Nigel drops before heading to the field with the rest of the team.

"The studio?" I ask, pissed that, yet again, my territory has been invaded. I feel like Califia. And, also like her, I'm about to wage war. "You can't come to the studio. What about your man?" I ask.

"What about yours?" she says. And just like that, I'm the one who's checked. But, not so fast.

"I'm actually bringing Jeremy this weekend. You should invite your man too and we can make it a little party," I say. I haven't invited Jeremy yet, but I was planning on it. I was going to wait and see how homecoming played out on Friday before saying anything to him though. But I'm sure he'll be game.

"Very funny, Jayd," she says, not amused. "This is our little secret, OK? Not even Nellie can know," Mickey says.

"Whose house?" Reid shouts through the bullhorn from the center of the makeshift stage in the middle of the field.

"Shark's house!" the crowd roars. We can't help but get swept away with the current.

"Whose house?" he yells again, wanting a louder response.

"Shark's house!" and, the music begins. The crowd goes wild as the ASB spirit squad comes out dancing to the marching band's vibrant beat. I love pep rallies. When I was a member of ASB, I was on the spirit squad. I even wore the lady shark mascot last year, and Reid was, of course, the male. But, I'm sure he's turned that job over to someone else, now that he's taken on deeper waters and bigger prey as president this year.

After the first performance by ASB, the rest of the week's activities are announced. The athletes and cheerleaders will have a step show tomorrow after the tug-of-war and South Bay history challenge. Chance and I perform for the Drama Club on Wednesday, after the potato sack and egg race, with Thursday left for the awards presentation for the week's activities and the pre-pep rally for the homecoming game on Friday.

"Do you think Nellie's going to win?" Mickey says, as we move with the crowd toward fifth period.

"As her campaign manger I have to say yes," I say. What a joke. My own candidate is treating me like crap. I guess Ms. Toni was right about this manager job being political.

"Yeah, but do you really think she has a chance at winning?" Mickey says, looking for Nigel in the crowd. I don't even bother looking for Jeremy, who informed me in the class this morning he wouldn't be attending. Instead, he, Matt, and Seth went to eat off campus, as usual. He has no school spirit at all.

"If transforming into a complete bitch to get the crown is an indicator of success, then yes. She has an excellent chance at winning," I say, noticing Nellie hanging with Tania and the other Drama candidates on the field with the football players. Nigel's down there with her. But, as soon as he sees Mickey and me, he leaves her and heads our way, making Nellie look right at us. I hope she doesn't think he's coming up here to see me.

Before he reaches us, Nellie heads off the field and toward the girls locker room, following Tania and Tania's friends. I wish she could see I'm not her enemy and that those girls just might be. They're the kind to sabotage a member of their own crew over jealousy. And she has to remember that Tania's a hater of mine, making herself a potential hater victim by association. Nellie's just lost all sense of reason going after this damn crown. I can't wait until this week's over.

Just as we think we've seen the last performance of the day and head to fifth period, a small crowd circles around the main lunch quad, near South Central. As Mickey, Nigel, and I head over to see what all the commotion's about, KJ's loud voice can be heard, leading a chant.

"Whose house?" he says, but in a slightly deeper voice than Reid's and with a completely different rhythm.

"Our house!" the other athletes respond from behind him,

forming a single line. Then, Kendra, the lead cheerleader and the only Black girl on the varsity squad this year, hollers back.

"Whose house?" she says, leading the rest of the cheerleaders in a single-file line, next to the Athletes.

"Our house!" And the mini step show begins.

"Show-offs," I say, hating they used today as a preview for their show tomorrow. I have to admit, they're good. It was a smart campaign move, though. Now, everyone's going to be all hyped about the step show tomorrow, keeping the athletes' and cheerleaders' candidates in their heads, just like ASB does with every pep rally they get to host. Drama Club always gets the least exposure just by the nature of the campus's social structure. But usually we only need one shot to win over an audience.

When Chance and I perform together, we're just that good. And, with the help of the stage crew and Seth's creative set design, our show is going to be off the chain. We have rehearsal scheduled every day after school and before school on Wednesday morning. Chance is a great performer and I'm pretty good and we're both fast learners. Alia choreographed our routine and Matt and Leslie wrote the script, setting up the stage so we're inside a club. We are going to get this party started and show them whose house this really is.

~ 13 ~
Hate Mail

*"Put together a million man march
With some gangsta shit."*

—SNOOP DOGG/TUPAC

The next morning I decide to go to the library at break and get started on my English paper due next week rather than look for my girls or Jeremy. I'm exhausted with all of them. Just my luck, Misty is sitting next to the only available computer and I don't have time to come back any other day this week since we're rehearsing at lunch and after school for the next two days. I guess even big mouths have to study at some point.

"Hey, Jayd," Misty says, smacking on her Juicy Fruit. "How's the date hunt coming?" she says, taking her backpack out of the empty chair so I can sit down.

"Just fine. How are the leftovers?" I say, giving her a snide look. She's got too much confidence now, making her that much more annoying.

"Oh, they're good. Real good," she says, popping her gum and pissing off the librarian, who promptly shushes her.

"Whatever, Misty. I need to work so could you not talk to me for a good ten minutes, please," I plead. I have no time to waste this morning.

"Touchy, touchy. See, if you had a Black man you could work off some of that aggravation," she says, shaking her big hips in the small, wooden chair. She can be so nasty when she wants to be.

"Shut the hell up talking to me with all that bull," I say, trying to ignore her while surfing the Web. I log onto the Internet and check my e-mail, which is completely full. I don't have a computer at either my mom's or Mama's house. So, the only time I can get online is at school.

As Misty continues to send her hater rays my way, I sift through the many e-mails, stopping at one in particular. It has no sender and looks as if it's been forwarded to all the club lists at school with Nellie's name in the subject line. I wonder what this is. Maybe Seth sent out an anonymous flier promoting Nellie. When I open the picture I'm stunned to find a picture of Nellie changing clothes in the girl's locker room with Monifa's *Touch It* playing in the background. It's a full picture of her ass in a g-string. What the hell?

"Oh, shit," Misty says, spying over my shoulder. "Where did that come from?" she says. It's bad enough it's all over the Internet. Now Misty's going to have it all over school in no time.

"Misty, you can't tell anyone about this," I say, logging off the computer and picking up my bag, ready to bolt out the door. My paper will have to wait for another day. Right now I have to see who else knows about this and more importantly, if Nellie knows yet.

"Girl, I ain't got nothing to gain from spreading this around campus," Misty says, sounding sincere. "Besides, we both want the same thing for a change. The Black girl to win. And even though most of the dudes in South Central are athletes, we all want the same results," she says, sounding like she's got an idea. "If we find out who would benefit the most from Nellie's humiliation, then we'll also find out who did it," she says, looking like she's ready for a spy mission. How is it that Misty's offering to help me and my home girl is tripping? I feel like I'm in a warped reality.

"And how do you suppose we do that?" I ask, ready to leave her behind. I've got to get to Nellie before someone else does. I don't know if she's strong enough for this type of humiliation.

"If you'd listen for a minute I'll tell you," Misty says, slowing me down as I walk out the door toward South Central. "We can get all the athletes to put their ears to the ground. You know, locker rooms talk. And, that picture was apparently taken in the girl's locker room," Misty says, starting to make sense. If it's one thing she's good at it's scheming.

"So, you think they could find out who took the picture?" I ask. "Like anyone's going to fess up," I say, not really believing her plan will work.

"Oh, but they will if they haven't already."

"OK, Misty. See what you can find out in South Central and in the meantime I'll text Seth and ask him to take this off the web," I say, hardly believing I'm collaborating with Misty of all people. But, it's always better to have two cliques working together. There's just more power that way. And, if anyone can crack a computer code, it's Seth.

After plotting away break, I rush to third period, finding a sub in for Mrs. Peterson. This day is looking up after all. And, there's Jeremy waiting for me to sit next to him, in our usual seats.

"Hey, baby," he says, kissing me on my neck as I settle into my desk.

"You better stop that," I say, not really wanting him too. "You remember what happened last time you kissed my neck, Dracula," I say referring to the hickeys still prominent under my makeup. I wear it all day, even when I go to bed, to keep Mama from seeing.

"Don't tell me you're once bitten, twice shy, Jayd," he says, sitting back in his chair, looking ready for a good nap. The substitute is too busy trying to take roll and deal with students already asking for hall passes. I feel sorry for the subs at this school. White kids are the best hustlers when it comes to ditching. Speaking of which, the ditch queen herself, Tania and crew are next to approach the sub for a pass of their own, I assume.

"Hey, Jeremy," Tania says on her way to the teacher's desk, looking like she wants to take a bite out of him. "Checked your e-mail lately?" she says, passing up our desks while looking directly at me, even though she's supposedly talking to him. This broad knows something about Nellie's picture. I can feel it.

"No, why?" Jeremy says, taking out his cell phone, ready to pull up the Internet.

"Yeah, Tania, why should he check his e-mail?" I ask, ready to pounce on this heffa. If she had anything to do with Nellie's picture being e-mailed, I'm going to get wicked on her ass.

"Oh, no reason. Just thought he might like to see some new pics I noticed when I checked mine a little while ago," she says with a sinful grin on her face.

"What do you know about the picture?" I say, quickly rising from my seat and getting in her face. Her two homegirls step up a little closer, ready for whatever's about to go down. As fast as my blood's rushing, I could probably take all three of them down.

"Calm down, Little Kim," Tania says. "I don't know anything, except that your girl's campaign just went down the toilet and so did her reputation," she says, laughing with her girls.

"Why the hell is this funny to you?" I say, now yelling and causing the entire class to look our way. Jeremy, who's standing right behind me, grabs my arm, trying to get me to calm down. But, I'm just getting warmed up. "Aren't you and Nellie on the same team?" I say, reminding her they're both being sponsored by the Drama Club for homecoming court.

"Oh, come on, Jayd. Even you can't be that dense," she says, flipping her thick hair over her shoulder. If it's one thing I can't stand, it's a girl of any color trying to be White. She's about to get the shit slapped out of her and maybe some consciousness knocked in. "She's never going to win that crown. At least not as long as my girl Laura's running," Tania says, referring to Reid's girlfriend.

Oh, hell no. They're not friends, are they? Now, see what I say about these people up here being undercover haters. But wait until the folks in South Central find out about their little stunt. Then we'll see who's got the real power around here.

"OK, ladies," Jeremy says, sensing the volatile situation coming to a head. "Let's calm down. We don't need to get into this right now, do we?"

"The hell we don't," I say ready to throw the first blow. This heffa's been having it coming to her ever since she flirted with my man right in front of me. She's always throwing salt and now she's about to taste some on her lip.

"Do I need to call security, girls?" the aging male substitute says, as if he's really got any control. He's already pulled out two office referral slips. By the time he puts our names down, the fight will be over.

"What are you going to do, jump me?" Tania says, completely unaffected by my anger. This broad's gotten away with too much jaw jackin' in her day. It's time to let her feel the impact of her words. "Hitting me won't do anything, especially not help your friend with her little problem," Tania says, confident I won't hurt her.

"What exactly are you two talking about," Jeremy asks, completely unaware. He probably thinks it has something to do with him.

"She's talking about this," Tania says, pulling out her pink rhinestone covered blackberry, with the picture of Nellie on her screen.

"Damn," Jeremy says, staring at the picture of Nellie next to her gym locker, totally unaware of her picture being snapped. That's when I realize it could have just as easily been a girl who took the picture. Who else would have access to get that close with an unnoticeable camera in her phone, just like Tania's. This heffa's guilty and I know it.

"You stupid wench," I yell, snatching the electronic device out of her hand and smashing it to the ground.

"Shit," Tania screams, falling on the ground to pick up her cracked up blackberry. "You little hoodrat," she says. "You probably couldn't repay me for this if your whole family worked for a week," she says, two seconds shy of her face hitting the ground like her gadget did. Before I can pimp slap her like the trick she is, Jeremy intervenes.

"Come on, baby. Let's get some air," Jeremy says, catching me by both elbows and keeping me from attacking Tania, who's still on the floor.

"I don't want to get air. I want a confession," I say, trying to break free from Jeremy's tight grasp. "Just admit it, Tania. Be a woman about your shit," I yell as Jeremy picks me up and carries me out of the classroom into the empty hallway.

"Why are you defending her?" I yell at him. "Let me back in there so I can whip her ass like the trick she is."

"Jayd, calm down. You don't know if she did it or not," he says, still not letting me loose. "Do you want to be suspended again?" he says, trying to reason with me.

"What's going on out here," Mickey says, coming into the hallway. Nellie and Mickey's class isn't far from here and knowing them, they were running late from break. I didn't want to tell them like this. But, it's better now than later.

"Have y'all heard about Nellie's picture on the web?" I ask, trying to soften the blow for Nellie.

"Yeah, Seth told me he used the one of me from prom last year," she says, completely oblivious to what I'm about to say. Mickey, on the other hand, looks as if she already knows.

"She's not talking about that picture, Nellie," Mickey says, looking from me to Nellie, letting me break the bad news. As pissed as we both are at her for her behavior, she's still our girl and we don't like seeing her hurt.

"Nellie, someone took a picture of you changing in the girl's locker room and sent a mass e-mail." Nellie becomes the picture of pure rage. Now, this is new.

"I want to see it," Nellie says, looking around for the nearest computer, I assume.

"Here it is," Jeremy says, showing her the image he just downloaded onto his cell. Me and my girls have simple cell phones that don't do all of this new stuff. And, if they do, Mickey and I can't afford the extra expense and Nellie's parents wouldn't go for something that extravagant, so why bother knowing about it? "I'm sorry about this, Nellie," Jeremy says, looking as sorry as I feel.

"This was yesterday after lunch," she says. "I was changing out of my rally outfit and back into my school clothes." Maybe if she wasn't so damn vain in the first place she wouldn't be in this mess. But, we'll deal with her sins another time. Right now, vengeance is mine to take out on her enemies. "Who would want to do this to me?" she asks, like she hasn't made plenty of her own haters.

"I don't know for sure, but I've got a pretty good idea," I say. "Misty's trying to find out if anyone said anything in the boy's locker room. But, I think Tania had something to do with it."

"You don't know that for sure," Jeremy says, again defending the broad. What's up with that? He's my man now. He's supposed to be down with me unconditionally. Not reasoning with the opposition, even if it is his ex lover.

"Yes, I do," I say, rolling my eyes and neck at him and looking at Nellie, who doesn't seem convinced of my accusations either.

"Why would you say that?" Nellie says, as if it's not at all possible.

"Well, first of all, she was with you yesterday in the locker room," I say, remembering them walking off the field together after the rally ended. "Also, she was the one who broke the news in government class a few minutes ago," I say. I can't believe I have to defend myself against Tania after I was ready to throw blows with her over Nellie's reputation. Ain't this some twisted BS.

"But, none of that proves she would do something like this," Nellie says, disgusting me and Mickey, who looks like she's had enough, for real this time.

"OK," Mickey says, putting her hands on her hips, demanding Nellie's full attention. "What about the fact that Tania's your homegirl's man's ex and might hate on you just because she's a bitch like that?" she says, stating the obvious missing element to the list of why Tania's the natural suspect. Even Jeremy looks convinced now.

"Everything's not always about Jayd," Nellie says, sounding just like she did the other day when she was talking about Nigel being my homecoming date. This girl is too much. Why is she hating on me like this? "Besides, Tania's too classy to do something like this," she says, pushing Jeremy's cell away from her eyes, as if not seeing it will mean it doesn't exist.

"Nellie, you can't be serious," I say, now pissed at her way more than I was at Tania a moment ago. "Tania told us she wants Laura, her friend and your competition, to win."

"That's ridiculous. She just said that so she wouldn't hurt Laura's feelings. Think about it," she says, looking at the three of us, all looking at her like she's stupid. "Why would she do this? She's on my team. The goal is for all the club's nominees to be chosen for the court. Wouldn't that be perfect?"

"Nellie, you sound like you've been brainwashed or something," Mickey says. And, she's right. Popularity and crowns can do that to anyone who wants either one bad enough. But, combine them both and you've got an explosion on your hands, which is what we've got here with Nellie. Whether she knows it or not, her enemy is in her camp and determined to humiliate her. I have a feeling this was the precursor to my dream about Nellie's homecoming disaster. And, Mama, the only person who can help me determine my next step, is still upset with me. It's going to take more than a spell to get Nellie and Mama back on my team.

~ 14 ~
Mama's Magic

"Take a lot more than you
To get rid of me."

—EVE

It's Tuesday afternoon and Mama's been pissed at me for over a week now. But, she's going to have to get over it. I need her help to get through tomorrow's performance and the rest of the week. When I get home, she's in the kitchen making tea cakes, and I'm just in time to help her cut the dough.

Walking into the dingy yellow kitchen, I see Mama's in her white housedress, pink, tattered house slippers and a white scarf, covering her freshly cornrowed hair tied neatly in a bun at the base of her neck. I like when Mama wears her hair like me. She taught me how to cornrow my hair when I was about five years old. Mama says braiding your hair into different patterns sends different messages to your Ori, or your divine path. She alternates between this hairstyle and the French Twist, opting for cornrows when her spirit needs healing.

This is the first time she's been able to cook since our plumbing disaster. When I got home Sunday evening, the bathroom was back to normal and Mama's mood has been lightening ever since. After Netta does her hair she looks radiant, as if she's released all of the anger she's been holding in. Thank God, because I sure could use a hug.

"Hey, baby," she says, putting down the sifter full of cinnamon and sugar to give me a hug. She smells like sweet buttermilk and flour. By the looks of it, she's been baking all afternoon. It's almost six in the evening and she's on her fifth dozen.

"Who are you baking for this time?" I ask, walking over to the sink to wash my hands before taking my customary seat at the kitchen table.

"For you," she says, picking up the sifter and shaking the contents over the flattened dough. "I thought it might help with your dancing tomorrow," she says, cutting the glazed dough into small squares. "You and your friends will need the carbs, no?" she says, placing the cakes onto the parchment paper in four neat rows.

"I'm not going to say no to tea cakes and I'm sure they'll appreciate them, too. Thank you," I say, taking one from the fresh pile cooling on the table and stuffing the entire thing into my mouth. My friends will be lucky if they each get one. These are my favorite treats.

"Did you find a date for the dance?" Mama says, making small talk while the last batch bakes. It smells so good in here, completely covering the scent of broken toilets and funky men. Mama's good at making it feel warm and clean again. She heals through this kitchen.

"Yes. Myself," I say, on my second cake. "I'm going stag." I'm officially done trying to get a date for the dance. Sometimes a girl has to stroll by herself. And now is definitely one of those times. I made my decision after Jeremy and I talked about it last time. I don't need anymore drama where dudes are concerned. And, the only way I can see that happening is if I don't have a date.

"That's my girl," Mama says, cracking a smile before taking the hot sheet of golden sweets out of the oven. Damn, she's good. If Jeremy had one of Mama's cookies, he'd probably do anything she asked him too.

"And, how's Raheem?" Mama asks, taking me back to Friday's session. He's so sure of himself, it's frightening. And, I'm not so sure if I'm completely over Raheem, which isn't a good thing if I'm pledging myself to another man.

"Raheem's fine," I say, taking the Ziploc bags out of the cupboard to store the tea cakes that have cooled.

"We'd better put these in our room so nobody gets to them," Mama says, taking a couple of bags and filling them, careful not to smash a single cake. "You know how your Daddy likes his treats," she says, leading the way to her bedroom. I don't think she's talking about tea cakes. Daddy's more of a cobbler man. Mama's always salty about Daddy's girlfriends.

"Mama, how come Williams women can't seem to keep a man?" I blurt out. She's clearing off her desk on her side of the room, making room for the cakes. We usually store anything we want to save in here. The boys don't dare come into Mama's room.

"Is that one of the lessons you've written down from Maman's history?" she asks before sitting down on her bed. She takes an old church fan with her and Daddy's picture on it and cools her glistening forehead while laying back on her pillows. "If so, it needs rephrasing," she says, searching for her herbs and water glass with her eyes. I follow her gaze to the nightstand, anticipating my need to get up and prepare her evening concoction.

"Rephrasing how?" I ask, retrieving the glass and pouch before heading to the kitchen.

"You said it as if we don't have the power. Girl, haven't you learned anything about our legacy?" she asks as I walk back into the room with her thick drink.

"Well, actually, I have been reading a lot about Maman's relationship with Jon Paul," I say, taking a seat on my bed and reaching to grab my spirit notebook from the side of the bed where I hide all my books, magazines, letters, and other things someone might mistake for scratch paper or a coaster. "And, it seems she cheated on him with his best friend, Pierre, a White man," I say, recalling last night's reading.

"Yes, go on," Mama says, swallowing the last of her herbs and settling back in bed, ready to be impressed.

"So, how come Maman cheated on Jon Paul? Why can't we ever be happy with one man?" I ask, realizing we are all walking on the same path of heartbreak after all.

"Did you read anything about how controlling Jon Paul was with Maman or how she was the one the community came to with their problems, including Jon Paul's people?" Mama says, sitting up to look at me. "Jayd, it's not that we can't keep men. It's that men can't keep us," she says, smiling seductively. It's the same look my mother had on her face when she was talking to Jeremy the other night. The flirt before the sting. "You say it as if we want the men who want us, and that's not always the case."

"Well, I can testify to that," I say becoming a little too comfortable. I always have to remember Mama's my elder, not my homegirl, no matter how cool she can be. "Well, then why didn't Maman leave before Jon Paul killed her? Why didn't she just be with Pierre?" I ask, knowing life isn't always that simple.

"Oh, girl, you talk like you don't know what the hell love is," she says, becoming impatient with my line of questioning. "Besides, times were different then. And, Maman was very tied to the community. She couldn't just leave them behind. So, she stayed and continued to work as his wife. Because that's what marriage is without love: free labor," she says, massaging her hands with oil.

"I thought they were in love," I say, reviewing my notes. "It was a deep, pervasive, intoxicating love, from what I jotted down," I say, reading my quotes.

"Yes, at first. But, as soon as he became jealous of her power and started that possessive crap, love went out the door." Mama takes the spirit book from the nightstand where I left it after last night's reading and turns to Maman's story. "Did you notice the bath she gave herself when she was dealing with Pierre?" Mama says, alluding to my problem with Raheem.

"Mama, I've got bigger problems," I say, needing to ask her about Nellie's situation. "There's a picture going around of Nellie getting undressed in the girl's locker room and I think Jeremy's ex is behind it." Mama looks up from the big book, horrified.

"Poor girl," Mama says, looking worried for Nellie. "And she probably doesn't know who her enemies are, does she?" Mama says, as if she was at school when it happened.

"Not at all. She wants so badly to win this crown and be in the popular crowd she won't believe me. But, I know that wench did it," I say, wishing I'd slapped Tania when I had the chance.

"And, so, what are you going to do?" Mama says, looking at me as if to say I'm on my own with this one.

"Well, I was kind of hoping you could help me in that department," I say, getting up to sit on the edge of her bed and hugging her legs. I used to sleep like this when I had nightmares as a little girl. As soon as I'd touch Mama's legs, all the bad thoughts would leave my head. But now, it's not that easy.

"Oh, Jayd. I've told you time and time again, everything you need to solve all of your problems is already within you. Call on your powers, child, and your path will be cleared." She gently runs her freshly painted nails through my hair. "If

Nellie won't listen to you, pray that she gets the message another way. Remember, it's not about your victory, but hers. Take yourself out of the equation and you will have a greater perspective of the situation."

"But, I'm too close to it," I say. "How can I separate myself when I'm all up in the mix? It's my friends, my club, my man's ex, and I'm the campaign manager. Where am I going?" I say as Mama shoos me off her legs, swinging them to the side of her bed where her altar rests.

The altar is the family shrine for the women in the household. The five-tiered white shelf is filled with pictures of our deity, Oshune, Mama's ancestors, pictures of me and my mother, my auntie and uncles, and many other family and friends. There's food, candles, and other things covering each tier, making it appear cluttered to the outside eye. A visitor probably wouldn't even know it was in here, protected under a white veil in the corner of the room, between her bed and the window. There's hardly any space for Mama to kneel before it. But she does, at least twice a day.

"Pray to the ancestors. My legacy is yours to call on." She takes a picture of Maman from the altar and hands it to me, telling me to concentrate on the eyes of the ancient face.

"The women in my father's family loved Maman. They served her as they would a queen, and so did the women in the community. When Maman died, they took me in, caring for me and showing me what a mother's love can do and how a spirit transcends physical death. Maman was there. She was always there. She never left, just came back in different ways through different people."

"If you grew up with your father's people, how did you learn about your mother's lineage?" I ask, slightly confused.

"Like I said, Jayd. Maman is a queen, and the stories of queens are recorded," she says, tapping her journal. "All of the women in our legacy have journals. This is where your power lies, child. In your words. Have you been recording your dreams?" she asks. I look at her ashamed, shaking my head no.

"Jayd, girl. When are you going to listen to me? You know how to deal with your problems, but won't take the time to do it. Get your notebook and write down Maman's bath prescription for direction and knowledge of following the right path," she says, pointing to the page with a picture of Maman in the bathtub, her long hair piled on top of her head, soaking to her neck. The sketch is lifelike, with the image almost jumping from the page. Whoever wrote Maman's story did so with love and meticulous affection.

"Who drew the pictures?" I ask as I record the list of candles, herbs, oils, and other ingredients for the bath.

"Your great-aunts, my father's sisters. Although they were older than Maman, they also became her first goddaughters. It was these women who kept Maman's spirit alive and taught me to do the same," she says, looking from the book to my journal, making sure I'm recording properly.

"I got it," I say, tucking my journal into my chest, not allowing her to see.

"Yes, you do, Jayd. Now, go and put it to good use. Help your friend, Jayd. Poor, lost Nellie," Mama says, turning on *Jeopardy* and pointing me out of her room. "If anyone ever needed Oshune's mercy, it's that girl. Now, go ask her for it." Mama's right, this isn't about me and Tania or me and Nigel and Raheem or me and anyone else. It's about Nellie. Now, if I could just get her to see that before she's completely blindsided again.

After praying and bathing the rest of my evening away, one plan is revealed to me. If I could get Nellie to perform with us, being Seth's girl on the last hook of Jay-Z's song, then it might win her back some respect. And, I don't care if she has stage fright. The best thing to do in these types of situations is to sway the crowd. And, that's just what I intend for us to do.

"Hey, Mickey, have you seen Nellie this morning?" I ask as I pass Mickey at her locker on the way to mine. I can't believe it's already the Wednesday before homecoming, but I can't worry about that right now. I need to put up these tea cakes and my outfit for the performance today and get my Spanish and English book out. Jeremy dropped me off at the front door today so I could get to my locker a few minutes early. Nellie's not returning any of my messages and I really want her to come to the last rehearsal.

"No, and I don't want to. She's gone too far this time," Mickey says, still pissed at yesterday's betrayal. "How could she not believe you when you told her about Tania's stunt? If it were me, I would have beaten Tania's ass down all day and took you to Hometown Buffet afterwards." Mickey is crazy, but I love her loyal spirit. .

"Nellie is a bit special and don't act like you don't know," I say, reminding her that Nellie's her friend too. And, friends don't turn on each other, no matter how ugly they can get. "Remember, she has some good qualities too. Although, humility ain't nowhere on the list," I say, getting a smile out of Mickey. "If you see her, please tell her to meet us in the drama room for rehearsal at break. It's important. And here, have one," I say, sharing my treats with her. I open the bag, revealing the freshly baked cakes. She grabs one and takes a big bite.

"Damn, Jayd. These are slamming. Did you make these?" she asks, digging into my bag and stealing two more before I can close it.

"No, Mama did. And, no more. They're for Chance and Seth too. I'll see you later," I say, heading toward my locker.

"Alright. And, good luck if I don't see you before lunch," she says, devouring another tea cake. I've got to get word to Nellie to be at rehearsal. Maybe Chance can get to her. As I scroll down my phone book to text Chance, Reid walks right into me, almost knocking me down.

"What the hell was that?" I yell at him, causing the few people in the hall to stop and stare.

"Oh, I'm sorry, Jayd. I didn't see you," he says with a straight face. I think this fool did it on purpose. I know he's not trying to physically intimidate me. I'll sick Jeremy's ass on him so fast he won't know what hit him.

"You need to watch yourself, punk," I say, rolling my neck and walking back up toward the hall.

"I'd save the little warning for your friend," Reid says, meaning Nellie, I assume. I turn around, walking back toward Reid, with everyone's eyes on me. I know some of these people up here must think I'm a loose cannon. But, somebody has to check these White folks and if it's got to be me, then so be it.

"I know Laura's not really all that good-looking and she wouldn't have any friends if it weren't for her money," I say, getting up in Reid's face. "But, to pull a stunt like e-mailing naked pictures of an innocent girl, she must be really desperate. And, so must you." Every blue and purple vein in Reid's forehead looks like it's about to burst all over his tanned flesh. If I didn't already know he must be involved in sabotaging our campaign somehow, his reaction would scream his guilt.

"You don't know what you're getting yourself into, Jayd," he says, looking like he wants to punch me. "Watch who you make accusations against," he says, boldly threatening me in front of anyone within earshot.

"Careful there, Mr. ASB president. Some would say taking pictures like that, as well as sending them, could be considered a felony. And, you threatening me isn't going to help your case," I say, really pulling his chain. Just as I'm on a roll, the first bell rings and the Main Hall's suddenly inundated with students and teachers rushing about. I still have to get to my locker before class and Reid hasn't moved a muscle, waiting on my next move. Remembering one of the lessons from both Maman and Califia, I decide it best not to reveal all of my intentions, leaving room for surprise.

"Whatever you're thinking about doing Jayd, think real hard. Ask your boyfriend what happens when you mess with the Connelly brothers and their girls," he says, thinking he's telling me something I don't already know.

"Everyone has their secrets, Reid. And, yours don't scare me." What he doesn't know is my legacy is stronger than Jeremy's or his, and I know that. Now, it's time to show them who the reigning queen is up in this place is, with or without a crown.

~ 15 ~
Coming Home

"Relying on talent,
Not marketing and promotion."

—KRS-ONE

Thursday is finally here and for the first time in days I feel absolutely confident in what I'm doing. We are going to win best performance and check Reid's ego. It's a shoe-in for Nellie's crown. Besides, anytime I'm with Chance is like going home, whether we're on or off stage. Matt was right about us having a spark when we perform together, even if Jeremy doesn't like it.

With each rehearsal me and Chance's performance gets tighter. Our skit is sassy and quick, just enough to serve as the perfect intro into our rap. I think Matt told Leslie our conversation about cookies and cheddar verbatim, because our lines sound as if they came from Chance and me directly. All we had to get down was our timing in the rhyme: Jay-Z's flow is tight and not easy to emulate, but Chance is up for the task. And, after today's rehearsal, I know we're going to turn this school out.

"There's my Beyonce," Chance says, looking like he just stepped out of a Jay-Z video. He really gets into whatever part he plays, which in this case is a baller/pimp. I love it.

"Have you been wearing that all morning?" I ask, flicking his heavy platinum chain, Rocawear sweats, and shirt. He usually doesn't wear his chain to school. But, I guess he wanted to be as accurate as possible.

"Careful with the bling, baby. Daddy will get you one if you're good today," he says, hitting me on the behind, taking his role a bit too far.

"Chance, you better watch it," I say smacking his hand hard. "I know Matt suggested *Can I Get A* . . . because of our little conversation at his party a few weeks ago, but you ain't really a pimp."

"Oh, isn't this cute?" Nellie says, startling us both. I see she got my message. Mickey's not with her. She, I'm sure, didn't want to accompany Nellie down here. She has no interest in seeing the Drama area, and neither did Nellie until now.

"Hey, Nellie. We were just starting to rehearse," I say, hoping she doesn't think it's more than it is. "I'm glad you're here." Matt and Seth enter the room behind Nellie, ready to cue the music and get us started. We have enough time for at least three full run-throughs. And, because we're a club performing, we get a pass from fourth period to rehearse before the show.

"What's this about me being in the show?" she says, walking in as if she has some authority over our space. Matt and Seth look at each other, amused by the diva in the room.

"We want you to be in the last part with Seth as his girl. You just need to dance along while he rhymes. It'll be good to show that you're unscathed by the picture going around." As if she's hearing the bad news for the first time, Nellie breaks down in tears.

"Why would someone do this to me?" Nellie says, breaking the record for a delayed reaction. Quick to lend a shoulder and whatever else he can offer, Chance rushes over to hug Nellie.

"Don't worry, Nellie. We're going to win and find out who

did this to you," Chance says, reassuring a fractured Nellie. I'm glad it's finally setting in.

"I still don't believe it was Tania," Nellie says.

"Unbelievable," I say, throwing my hands up in disbelief. "What will it take for you to get it? Them shooting you with paintballs?" I say, letting one of my dreams slip.

"What are you talking about?" Nellie asks.

"Nellie, trust me. Tania and her crew don't care about you at all. Reid basically admitted to having something to do with this and Laura and Tania are girls," I say.

"That skanky ass bitch," Chance says, feeling his character a little too much.

"Careful there, White boy," I say walking over to where he and Nellie are standing and offering them both a tea cake from the bag in my backpack. "I'm sorry this is happening to you. Really, I am," I say, not wanting to be unsympathetic to my friend, but I'm more than tired of her princess act. "But, we need to win," I say, pulling Chance to the center of the room. I hand the cookies to Matt while he and Seth set up the sound-system and Chance and I practice our brief intro. Jay Z's hard beat blares through the surround sound speakers in the ceiling. We all immediately begin to bounce just because it sounds so good. Chance and I grab the hand held microphones from their stands and begin our duet.

Nellie, a Jay-Z fan on the low, starts to bounce, feeling our routine. Other drama heads start to float in to watch us perform. Chance and I, who are now feeling our own vibe, start to lead the small crowd in the hook, bouncing our shoulders up and down and I start my part.

"You ain't gotta be rich, but bump that," I say, dancing along to the bass line. I love this shit. When it's time for Seth's turn to rap Jah Rule's hook, I pull Nellie onto the stage, which she initially resists, but is encouraged by the other students to join in. Like a natural video vixen, Nellie dances with Seth's flow, making a perfect end to our routine. By the time it's over, everyone in the room is bouncing and grooving. We've turned it into a party in here. Now, if we could just do the same at lunch we'll have a good shot at winning best-in-show and Nellie's crown.

"I thought this was a rehearsal, not a club," Jeremy says into my ear, catching me off guard.

"What's up, man?" Chance says, leaving me to go dance with Nellie. Everyone's having a good time.

"When did you get here?" I say, leading him outside the animated room. I'm fanning myself like a church lady and could use some fresh air. We stop outside the door and lean up against the wall, cooling in the shade. It's another hot October day. I'll be so glad when this month is over in a couple of days. Maybe the weather and the drama will chill out.

"Damn, girl, you look like you just ran a mile," he says, wiping a few beads of sweat from my forehead. Looking down at me with a smile, Jeremy pulls me in close to him and kisses me. "Even JLo doesn't rehearse this hard."

"Oh, yes she does if she wants to be the best, which is exactly what Chance and I are." As soon as I let the words out of my mouth, I regret it. Jeremy looks at me hard, like he wants to say something smart, but doesn't. How does he control his actions like that? Man, I wish I had some of his power.

"Yeah, well I'm going to take off. I've had enough of the homecoming hype," he says, pulling away from me.

"What?" I exclaim. If the music wasn't so loud, I'm sure everyone in the drama room would have heard me. "You're not going to stay and watch us perform?"

"I just did," he says. "Besides, I know you two will win, hands down," he says, forcing a slight smile. "I have complete faith in you." Ah, damn, as if I didn't feel bad enough about the whole Nigel and Raheem situation, now he lays more guilt on me.

"It would be nice to see your face in the crowd for support while I'm on stage," I say, reclaiming my spot in his arms. He bends down, kissing my forehead and hugging me tight. God he smells fresh, like Irish Spring and Downy.

"You'll have to settle for seeing my face after school, because I'm out, baby. The beach calls," he says, giving me another kiss on the lips before leaving. "I'll meet you after school," Jeremy says as he walks toward the back parking lot. I'm very disappointed in Jeremy's aloof attitude. It's not as sexy as I thought it was a couple of weeks ago. Now it's just getting on my nerves. Well, the show must go on, with or without my man.

"Are y'all ready to go on?" Reid asks as Chance and I approach the stage. Seth and Matt have been here since third period setting up. We rehearsed all of fourth period, so we're more than ready. Reid's acting like nothing happened. But, after this is all over, I've got something for his ass.

"Yeah," Chance says, looking like he wants to beat the hell out of Reid. I hold his hand, letting him know there will be plenty of time for that later. Right now, we need to win the crowd.

"Let's do this," I say. I look up at Chance as Reid announces our club and nominees, Tania included. I have a quick hot flash and get a snapshot of my dream about Nellie and Chance getting blasted at homecoming. What the hell?

"Jayd, let's go," Chance says, pulling me back into reality. We're ready to do our thing. Leading me on stage, Chance begins our skit.

"So, what you're saying is, if I don't buy you nice gear, get your hair and nails done and pay your cell bill, you ain't giving up the cookies," he says, eliciting laughter and *hell yeahs* from the ladies in the large crowd. Damn near the whole school is present and we've just caught everyone's attention.

"Hell no you can't get at this. I treat myself like a queen," I say, gesturing toward our nominees on stage. "And, I expect to be treated like one by any dude who wants to step to me," I say, switching across stage and playing the roll of a girl with hella attitude, just like in our song. "And, for the record, my cookies ain't for sale." With my last line, Matt starts the music and the crowd erupts.

"Can I get a . . ." Chance starts the song off, but we can barely hear ourselves over the crowd's cheers. Everyone's rapping along to the beat, validating our choice in music. Chance and I keep performing, thriving off the crowd's energy. I still wish Jeremy's face was in the crowd. But, I see Mickey and Nigel vibing in the front row and that's all the support I need.

Seth and Nellie join us at the end, and the crowd by now is hollering back at an electric pace. Our five-minute routine turns into a twenty minute party. After our performance, the crowd takes over the field, hyped to the fullest extent of a pep rally ever. Reid and Tania even get into the groove.

"That was the best performance yet," Seth says as we walk off the stage and toward the locker room to cool off.

"We won. I know it," Matt says, following Seth.

"Did you see the crowd? They're way too excited. You'd think it was a real concert by the way they responded," Chance says, still hyped and in full character. He gets a rush from performing, and so do I. I'm just being more low key about it than he is, and I'm tired. I can't wait to get home and get in my bed. I have a long day tomorrow and an even longer night. I'm excited about us winning the award tomorrow too. But, with my girl's naked picture going around school threatening her crown and Jeremy tripping, I can't get too hyped. There's still a lot of work to be done.

HOMECOMING

Wearing my perfect red dress and gold heels, I'm stand-ing up against the gym wall, alone and watching all the other couples enjoy the dance. Just as I'm ready to call it a night, a man's hand grabs mine, leading me onto the dance floor. His touch is familiar and I welcome his embrace.

As we glide across the dance floor, the lights dim and it's only us dancing to the slow music playing in the background. My partner, pulling me up slowly into a breathtaking, deep kiss, hungrily obliges my curious lips. After kissing for what feels like hours, I pull away and smile at my partner: It's Ra-heem.

Oh, hell no, not another dream of me and Rah kissing. What the hell?

After our performance yesterday, the Drama Club and all of our nominees are confident we'll win the award. But, one can never be too sure at this school. After voting for the final-ist for homecoming princesses and the queen at break, all I could do was think about seeing Jeremy. He didn't answer his phone last night and he wasn't at the bus stop waiting for me this morning. Then, he sent me a text saying he was run-ning late, but I think it's more than that. He wasn't in third period today and now I'm worried. I've been waiting all day for lunch to come and now that it's here, I can only think about one thing: Jeremy. He also said he was going off cam-pus for lunch and would see me after school. But, I want to see him now, just to make sure we're OK.

* * *

Instead of going to the awards ceremony straight from fourth period, I decide to look for Jeremy in the parking lot.

"Jeremy!" I call out, seeing him get into his Mustang, ready to pull off. I got here just in time.

"Jayd, what are you doing here? You're going to miss the awards," he says, turning down his music and putting the car into park.

"I know, but I had to say hi. I haven't seen you all day," I say, leaning into the open car window to give him a kiss. "What's up?"

"Nothing, Jayd. All this homecoming shit makes me sick. I'm just not into the dances and all," he says, repeating the same mantra I've heard for the past couple of weeks.

"It's not that bad, Jeremy," I say, tired of his selfish behavior. "I can understand not liking Reid for what he and his brothers did in the past. But, baby, you've got to let this go," I say, touching his forearm. "Besides, it's not about them. It's about us."

"Well, then since it's about us, why don't you forget the dance and go out with me tomorrow night," he says, challenging me. He knows I'm not about to give up homecoming to chill with him, no matter how sprung I am.

"Real funny," I say. "I've already risked accepting my award for you. Isn't that enough?" I ask.

"How do you know you won?" he asks. And, he's right: I don't. But, I'm sure I'll find out soon enough. "And, whether or not it's enough is up to you."

"What's that supposed to mean?" I ask, removing my hand from his arm and standing straight up.

"It means only you can decide whether or not you like me as I am. But, right now I'm going to grab something to eat before the bell rings. Go before you miss the entire ceremony," Jeremy says, starting his engine. "I'll see you after school," he says, pulling off, leaving me in a state of shock. What was that all about?

"*There are some soldiers in here, where they at?*"

Who's this texting me now?

"*We Won! Where r u?*"

Chance is right: Where am I? I feel like I'm in a relationship with a ghost. And, Jeremy's also right. I'll have to decide if this relationship is enough for me. But, not before the dance, because a sistah still needs a ride.

~ 16 ~
One Two Step

*"Now that I've got myself together baby/
And I'm having a ball."*

—MARVIN GAYE

Dances are among my mom's favorite high school memories. She's so exited about me going to homecoming tonight that she got off work early to pick me up from Mama's after Jeremy dropped me off at our regular spot. I left my dress at her house last weekend and already packed my other necessities. So, when she gets here we can leave right away, giving me plenty of time to get ready for my big night. I'm still hot at Jeremy for not going with me and for missing our performance. But, I'm tired of arguing and of the silence like we had this afternoon on our way home.

I'm exausted from the long week I've had, mostly spent dealing with Nellie's crap. She's still not fully convinced she should listen to me about Tania or the stunt they're planning for tonight. I spent all day yesterday trying to convince her without telling her I know she's in for it because of a dream I had a few weeks ago. I know she'd freak out if I'd said that. I even resorted to getting backup from Misty since Chance, Mickey, Jeremy, and I weren't enough.

Misty turned out to be pretty helpful in swaying Nellie's opinion in our favor, even though her mission to get concrete proof wasn't as successful. Because it wasn't done during an athletic event, no athletes or cheerleaders know anything about it. However, I know what needs to be done to reveal our enemies.

"Jayd, remember to take your notebook with you. Your assignment is due on Sunday," Mama says from her room, not letting me enjoy a moment free from worrying about more work. I actually almost did forget it, but she doesn't have to know that.

"No, Mama. I was just coming to get it," I say, walking in from the living room to retrieve the book from the nightstand.

"Just for lying to me, I'm not giving you your surprise," Mama says, displaying a small, green box with the letter *J* engraved on the top. It looks worn, like it's been around for a long time.

"What's this?" I say, excited Mama's sharing something special with me. I'm just happy she's in a good mood. I hate it when she's mad at me. Now I know better than to get on her bad side like that again.

"These bracelets have been in our family for generations," Mama says, opening the box to reveal five brass and jade bracelets. "The name Jayd goes back to Maman's time, when she took on the title of Queen Jayd upon her initiation into the priesthood," Mama says, taking the bracelets out of the box and motioning for me to sit next to her on the bed.

"Maman took on the name Jayd not only because we're known to have green eyes, but also because of the power the actual stone possesses." Slipping the bangles onto my right arm one by one, she tells me all about the mystical properties of the green stone.

"Jade is known to some as a stone of fidelity, bringing realization to a person's true potential and purpose in life. It is also known as a dream stone, improving the ability to remember dreams as well as assisting in their interpretation. It can also be used to release suppressed emotions through the dream process." That last meaning really hit home for me. Last night my dream of Raheem kissing me returned in full effect. Maybe I'm suppressing some emotions about him I need to deal with. Placing the last bracelet on my arm, Mama continues with the impromptu ceremony.

"This powerful stone also helps you to tune in to the needs of others and inspires wisdom when dealing with problems, like your current ones with Nellie. It also provides confidence. So, like I've told you before, Jayd. You have nothing to fear. The blood flowing through your veins is stronger than any enemy out there," she says, gesturing to the outside world.

"Wear these bracelets with care, child, as they are also delicate. Your great grandmother wore them, I wore them and now you wear them," Mama says, bringing my hands up to intercept her kiss. "Jade is also used to assist one in accessing the ancestor world. These bracelets are said to have brought Maman a gentle transition from the physical world to the spiritual world."

"Mama, why are you giving me these to wear tonight? It's a dance, not a marriage," I say, feeling like she's taking this way too seriously. Without thinking, I take my hands away from hers and play with the bangles, causing them to move out of the order Mama placed them in.

"Pay attention to the positioning of fragile things, child," she says, reclaiming my arms and repositioning each bracelet. As she does this, I remember my brief hot flash yesterday. Mama knows more than she's letting on, as usual. But, I get the message nonetheless. I need to be more aware if I want to help Nellie make it through tonight.

"Oh, Jayd, you look gorgeous in red," my mom says, admiring my reflection in her mirror. She helped me put my hair up in a cascading ponytail and did my makeup. She loves playing dress-up.

"Thank you," I say proudly. Even though I still think Jeremy's wrong for not taking me to the dance, he more than made up for it by buying me this dress. My mom still doesn't understand and hates me going alone. She's just glad Jeremy's going to be my ride for the evening.

"That boy is stupid," my mom says, handing me my gold heels from the closet. "Why would he want to buy you the dress, take you, and pick you up but not actually go to the damn dance?"

"It's very personal to him," I say, not wanting to give up the entire story right now. At least I'll be too preoccupied with saving Nellie's behind to worry about Jeremy's absence. I've left her several explicit messages on how we're going to handle the paintball situation. She's yet to call me back and confirm she received any of the messages, but I'm sure she did. And, I hope they sink in.

"There's you're silly little boyfriend now," my mom says, responding to the doorbell and passing me by to open the door for Jeremy. I take one last look at myself in the mirror. I know I'm overdressed to play *The Bodyguard* tonight, but I'm dressed just right to have a good time. And, with Raheem, Nigel, and my homegirls there, I'm sure we'll have our fun, even amidst all the drama.

As we approach the top of the football field a half hour into the game, Jeremy's still in silent mode and I look too good to care. When I step out of the car, he reaches down to give me a kiss before closing the door behind me.

"You look gorgeous, girl," he says, half smiling. But, even with the comment breaking his silent treatment, there's something especially sad in his eyes tonight. "I'll see you after the dance."

"Jeremy, wait," I say, feeling like it's my first day at kindergarten and I don't want my mom to leave me. "Can't you at least stay for the game?" I say. Before he can answer, Mickey walks up behind me, surprising me.

"Damn, Jayd, is that you? You look hot, girl," Mickey says, drawing attention from the other people hanging outside. I love that everyone dresses up for the football game and the dance right after. White folks do it their way, all day.

"Yeah, it's her," Jeremy says, smiling brightly. "I told you that you looked good."

"Hey, Jeremy. Are you staying for the game?" Mickey says, repeating my plea.

"No, I've got other plans. But, I'll be here to pick my queen up right after," he says, kissing me before getting into his car and leaving. Sensing my disappointment, Mickey takes me by the hand, escorting me through the gates and down the crowded bleachers. Feeling the buzz, I start to get excited. Everyone's dressed in their best and sitting in the bleachers. It's a funny sight to see and I'm glad to be a part of it.

"Where's your man?" I ask.

"Oh, he couldn't make it. His parole officer called him in yesterday afternoon and put him under house arrest for the weekend until he clears his drug test," she says. I don't know how she deals with all of her man's problems. Oh, yes I do: by occupying herself with other men.

"Girl, you missed it," Mickey says, leading us down the bleachers at lightening speed. "Nigel already scored two touchdowns and it's not even half time yet."

"I'm sure he's just getting started," I say as we finally settle into a spot in the front row. I can't help but look around, expecting to see people in hoods come out from under the bleacher, ready to attack. "How's the other team doing?"

"Don't you see that big zero on the scoreboard?" Mickey says, pointing toward the end zone. Damn.

"Have you seen Nellie?" I ask, looking around the crowded

field. I don't see Raheem. Chance is also nowhere in sight. But, I suspect wherever he is Nellie's not too far away.

"No, not yet. But, she left me a message saying she would be on the low until the coronation during the dance." Well, I guess that's good. At least I don't have to worry about saving her until later.

As predicted, we whipped our rival East Beach High's ass. The football games are anti-climactic, especially since we are the best out of all the beach-area schools, Westingle included. And, now that we have a Westingle brotha on our team, we're unstoppable.

Now basketball's another thing. I love the games because KJ and his boys hustle. And, the other teams hustle right back. But, football isn't as exciting. And with Nigel on the team, I know no other team can beat us. That's why the football players are especially cocky.

After the game, Mickey and I follow the crowd to the gym. Taking our time so she can wait for Nigel, we see the custodians begin setting up the field for the coronation. I wonder if my dream is off this time: Maybe nothing will go down. But, if history's taught me anything, it's that when I dream of drama it usually happens, one way or another. And, it's better to be safe than sorry.

"Hey, Nigel," Mickey says, practically leaping from our post by the gate and into his arms. "You were so good tonight," Mickey says, making my stomach curl.

"Good game," I say, giving Nigel a hug after Mickey lets him go. He's still a bit wet from his quick shower and smells good, reminding me of Rah's scent.

"Thanks, boo. Have you seen Raheem? He was supposed to meet me here after the game," Nigel says, looking around for him.

"No, I haven't," I say, feeling like he just read my mind.

"I'm going to chill out in my car for a minute before going to the dance. Want to come?" Chilling in the car is code for smoking a blunt, and I don't want to go inside smelling like weed.

"I'll pass," I say. "But, thanks for the thought."

"I'll join you," Mickey says, draping her arm around Nigel's waste. "See you in a little while, Jayd."

"And, when my boy gets here, make sure you keep him company," Nigel says as they head off toward the parking lot. Once Raheem sees me, I'm sure I'll have no choice.

Walking into the dimly lit, crowded gym turned disco dance floor, I spot Misty and KJ dancing up close. If I weren't in need of her help, I'd have to say something about her trifling behavior. But, we're on a tight schedule. The names for the winners of this morning's vote are going to be announced any minute. And, Nellie's on stage, in position.

"Misty," I say, breaking up the lusty couple. "I need your help." KJ, looks up from their embrace and takes me in. He's obviously pleased with my appearance.

"Jayd," he says. "You look fine, girl," which isn't what Misty wants to hear. I hope KJ's comment doesn't make her change her mind.

"Jayd, how do you know anything's going to happen?" she says, reclaiming KJ's waist. "I told you I couldn't find anything to prove Tania's really behind the pictures," she says, almost whispering so no one else hears our conversation. Other couples are on the dance floor, drifting along to Keisha Cole's slow vibe. I didn't need a dream to tell me Misty would chicken out. It's a pattern for her. And, now that she's got KJ the least bit interested in her, she isn't going anywhere.

"Misty, you know I need you to tell me when you see the two people in the crowd change into hooded shirts," I say. I still don't know exactly who they are, but this is how it played out in my dream. If I have someone on the look out, I can text Nellie exactly when to exchange places with Laura. I don't think she actually knows about this little stunt. This is all Reid's doing. So, she won't be looking out for them, just caught in the unfortunate crossfire. But, the crowd is too large for me to hunt alone. I need help.

"Look, Lara Croft, this is not the time or the place to be pulling your little weird-ass stunts," Misty says, falling back into step with an amused KJ, who hasn't stopped drooling over me since his comment.

"Fine, don't help. So much for being down with the cause," I say, leaving the two of them to make fools of themselves with each other. I guess Jeremy was right. Sometimes it is solely a physical attraction with people.

Say what? Cause I'm coming for that number one spot, my phone rings. I look at my phone's screen to indicate Raheem calling.

"Hello," I say, looking around the crowded room for any perpetrators. Before Rah can answer, our eyes meet and he smiles. The room suddenly seems smaller. Damn, he looks good.

"I like your dress," he says into the phone, walking toward me. I meet him halfway. Hanging up our cells, we embrace, falling into the beat of Aaliyah's version of the Marvin Gaye song, *Got to Give It Up.*

"I like your suit." He looks straight classy pimp in an all-white three-piece with a red shirt, handkerchief, and hat to match. The colors blend well with his dark cocoa skin. Underneath the hat, his hair's braided in cornrows, showing off his faultless African bone structure. To not be a couple, we sure do look like one.

"So, your boy really let you come alone," he says, putting his hands around my waist, locking me into our dance. We sway back and forth, living the true lyrics: I'm not here to stand up against the wall.

"Yeah, but he's picking me up. And, he bought this dress you like so much," I say, looking up at him as he clenches his teeth.

"Oh, really?" He doesn't sound convinced at all. But, I don't have time for this right now. I have to be on the look out. Raheem and I can pick this up after the coronation.

"Look, Rah. I need your help. I know for a fact Nellie's going to be blasted by three people on the field," I say, hoping he feels my sense of urgency. "I need your help to spot them. I don't know who they are. But, we'll know then because they'll come out in black sweatshirts with hoods and paintball guns. It'll be hard to spot folks in the crowd outside, but I know we can."

"All right, Jayd. I know enough to trust you when you get crazy like this," he says, smiling, reminding me of old times. He and Nigel were always down with my schemes.

"All right, cute couples, time for a break. Let's get some fresh air. Refreshments are set up outside and we're ready for the coronation," Reid says into the microphone. "Please make your way back outside and take a seat. We're ready to bring in the ladies."

When we get outside, the spread of food and drinks on the long table is incredible. But, unfortunately I don't have time to enjoy any of it right now. Mickey and Nigel still haven't resurfaced from their visit to his car, leaving me and Rah on our own.

"Check this shit out. It looks like an episode of *Fast Inc*.," Rah says, responding to the parade of classic cars entering the football field, driving toward the stage, just like in my dream. Chance's Nova, carrying the junior class candidates, is second in line. "These White boys know how to do it up here."

"OK folks, settle down," Reid says, trying to calm down the crowd. "Here's how it works. I'll announce the winners and only they will step onto the stage to receive their crowns. The other nominees will step out of and stand next to their cars so we can give them a big round of applause for being such good sports," he says, eliciting shouts from the crowd.

As the cars pull up, parallel to the stage, nominees can be seen through the rolled-down windows, ready to burst with excitement. And, Nellie's no exception.

"The homecoming court results are . . . drumroll please," Reid says, stirring the crowd. Raheem and I are scouting in opposite directions, waiting for the shooters to show.

"For freshman princess, the winner is Candice Sheryl." The young White girl screams at the top of her lungs, and the crowd is right along with her. She steps out of her car and walks up the five steps to accept her crown. The other candidates line the vehicle with sad faces, but still clap as their new princess is crowned.

"Your sophomore princess is, drumroll please," Reid stalls. "Mary Brillstein, come get this crown, girl," Reid says as yet another White girl claims her crown. Rah and I look at each other, still on the mission. It's Nellie's turn and according to my dream, this is when it's supposed to go down. I feel the same chill as I did in my dream. It's happening now. I can feel it.

"Junior class homecoming princess is," Reid says, taking his time to open the envelope, and looking around as if he's expecting something to happen. I follow Reid's nervous glances around the field, hoping to see what he does. But, I can't. I look at Raheem, who's now scouting from across the field. I reflexively touch the bangles on my arm and remember all of the qualities of the jade bracelets. I have to trust in my ability to interpret my dreams, no matter how things in reality may appear.

I send the text to Nellie, warning her to be aware of her surroundings, no matter whose name gets called. Laura, one of Nellie's competitors, is seated behind her in Chance's car.

"Your princess is, Nellie Smith." Nellie, completely absorbed in her excitement, steps out of the car behind Laura, who's visibly upset, waving like she's Mariah Carey. Nellie looks gorgeous in a cream, off-the-shoulder silk gown. I follow Laura's eyes toward Rah's spot in front of the bleachers across the field from where I'm standing. Catching my eyes, Rah follows my gaze and runs toward the spot.

Oblivious of the drama going on around her, Nellie proceeds up the steps to receive her crown. Reid nervously reaches for her crown on the pillow on the podium in front of him. Laura steps out of the line of fire, but not before Rah rushes the hooded perpetrators and inadvertently turns the aim in Laura's direction.

"Oh, shit," Reid says, dropping Nellie's crown to rush over to his girlfriend, who's now covered in blue paint. Nellie, shocked, looks right at me and gives me a look of recognition, letting me know she's sorry for doubting me. Tania and the rest of the crowd laugh at Laura as she wipes the paint out of her eyes, completely humiliated. The crowd is in an uproar. And Nellie, having picked up her crown from the podium herself, claims her title like the diva she is, with Chance right by her side.

Wrestling away from Rah, the gunmen escape off the field, followed by our handy security guards, Dan and Stan. Although we don't know exactly who tried to blast Nellie, our mission was still accomplished and my girl saved.

~ 17 ~
Social Session

*"From the pen he would scribe
On how to survive."*

—THE COUP

After Reid and Laura recover off stage, he reclaims the microphone and announces Tania as homecoming queen. Nellie, caught up in the drama, went with the rest of the homecoming groupies to take pictures with the photographer waiting off stage. I'm sure she'll spring for the most expensive package available.

Raheem and I get out of Dodge, not wanting to be in the dance pictures and school crowd, since it isn't his school and we're not really on a date, no matter how good we look together. I decide to show him around my school a little bit before the dance is over. With all of its faults, South Bay High has some of the best architecture and landscaping of any school I've ever been to. At night, it's a serene place to be.

"So, how did you know something was going down with your girl?" he says, casually grasping my hand as we walk up the hill to campus. Releasing my hand from his, I answer his question.

"I had a dream about it," I say, glad to share my secret with a friend. I've always been able to talk to Rah and Nigel about my gift, even though I didn't know what it was back in junior high. I just thought they were nightmares and I never told Mama or my mom about them. But, I could always tell Rah more about myself than anyone else, although not the complete details of my legacy. Our phone conversations were more stimulating than kissing sometimes. I miss vibing with him.

"You still having nightmares, girl?" he says, attempting to reclaim my hand. I'm flattered by his sweet gesture, but he knows I have a man and we can't be holding hands.

"They're more than that, and what are you doing?" I ask, snatching my hand away from his as he laughs, making me giggle too. "You know I have a man," I say, stepping a few feet away from him and turning back toward the gym.

"Yeah, that's true. And, I'm dating someone too." As always, he's honest about his shit, unlike KJ. Rah believes in soul mates and chicks on the side. As long as he's upfront about his, he feels he's doing the honorable thing. Dudes have some twisted logic sometimes.

"What the hell then? Stop trying to hold my hand and let's just enjoy the rest of the evening," I say, falling back into step with him. "I miss you too, Rah," I say, referring to his brief letter. "But we can only be friends, precisely because of your desire to have more than one woman. Is that a creed for all Muslim males?"

"No, smart ass," he says, shoving me with his shoulder. "But, I happen to be a young male, Muslim or not. And, you're a young female. I think we should be free to date other people, but still be in love with each other." Taking my hand into his, he lifts it to his lips and kisses my fingertips. His lips are so sweet they make me quiver. The jade bracelets fall down my arm, breaking the silence and forcing my dream of us kissing into my view. I pull my hand from his lips and look up at him, scared of his next move.

"We're not in love, Rah. We love each other, but we can't be in love," I say, envisioning us kissing. "It's been too long and I'm with Jeremy," I say, subconsciously touching the gold bangle on my other arm. "Let's go." As I lead the way back toward the dance, Raheem trails behind me without saying a word. Just what I need: another man giving me the silent treatment.

The line to take pictures is getting shorter and people are starting to leave. I'm sure there are plenty of after parties to go to, but I'm exhausted and still have to work in the morning. Ready to go, I walk Raheem to his car in the parking lot, running into Mickey and Nigel on the way out.

"Hey girl, what happened to y'all?" I ask, noticing they've missed damn near the entire dance.

"Oh, you know, lost track of time," Mickey says, smiling like Ms. Celie in *The Color Purple*. "Did Nellie win?"

"Yes, she did, and you would know that if you'd been there," I say, but Mickey's unscathed by my snide remark. Nigel takes Mickey by the waist and pulls her into him. If I didn't know better, I'd say the two of them are the ones in love.

"So, what's up with y'all?" Nigel asks. Raheem looks at me like he wants to say something smart, but doesn't. Jeremy should be here soon and I'm not sure how their first encounter's going to be. Jeremy will be cool, I know. But, Raheem's liable to do something stupid to assert his friendship with me.

"Beware of dudes who buy you a lot of shit, Jayd," he says, flicking the gold bangle hanging from my wrist and looking me up and down. His look makes me feel cheap.

"You bought me jewelry before," I say, recalling the gold nugget matching ring and pendant he bought me one Valentine's Day. Mickey and Nigel look at us, as well as other people walking around the lively parking lot. Some students are hanging out of their Escalades and Coopers, playing their music and drinking.

"Yeah, but at the right time. I didn't buy you outfits for

homecoming because that wasn't my responsibility. As your man, I was supposed to take you to the dance, which I did, always," he says. "I can't believe you're settling for some White dude who won't even take your fly ass to homecoming," he says, grabbing me around my waist and pulling me into his chest.

"Jayd, there's Jeremy's car," Mickey says, noticing the Mustang coming down the hill into the parking lot. Raheem holds me tighter while I try to wrestle myself out of his grasp, which just allows me to feel his chiseled body even more. There's electricity between us I can't explain. I knew he was going to start some shit.

"Rah, don't make a scene," I plead, unsure if he's hearing me or not. This man does what he wants and doesn't let anyone get in his way. But, he hasn't met Jeremy, who is also used to getting what he wants.

"This is the Raheem and Jayd I remember," Nigel says, laughing. "Where the hell y'all been?" he says, obviously amusing Mickey. Raheem and I aren't laughing.

"And, we were doing so well. I thought you wanted to be my friend," I say, hoping to get Raheem to see the situation my way.

"Jayd, we'll always be friends. But I love you too much to front, girl. These niggas up here and your White dude are some punks. And, you're much better than any of these fools. You need to check yourself," he says, touching the lower back of my dress as Jeremy pulls up to us.

"Hey, Jeremy," I say, stepping away from Rah and walking up to the car, ready to go. Raheem's got me all riled up and now I'm feeling confused again. All I can think about is my other dream of him kissing me. I'm glad Jeremy's here to stop it from coming true.

"Hey, baby," he says, getting out of the still-running car to open my door. "Hey, Mickey. How was the dance?" he asks, giving me a hug and kiss.

"It was OK. I'll fill you in on the details later," I say, not wanting to get him and Raheem any reason to talk for long. "These are my friends Raheem and Nigel," I say, awkwardly introducing them.

"Peace, man," Nigel says, not letting go of Mickey for a second.

"What's up, man," Raheem says, offering his hand to Jeremy, who shakes it firmly. "Jayd was telling me you like hip hop," he says, lying. I never told him that. This is so typical of Rah. He's such a hater.

"Yeah, I do. I actually like a lot of different styles of music. But, hip hop is definitely one of my favorites," Jeremy says, leaning up against the car. Where is Rah going with this?

"Has Jayd invited you to the studio yet?" Raheem says, smiling at me slyly. I was going to invite Jeremy myself, but he beat me to the punch. This can't be good. What's he up to now?

"No, she hasn't," Jeremy looks at me, trying to gauge my response. Before I can say anything, Raheem continues setting his trap.

"You two should come by tomorrow night. We're having a social session, where we listen to what we've got recorded for the demo so far," Raheem says.

"I was going to tell you about it on the way home," I say, feeling the need to explain myself. Nigel and Mickey look at me, shaking their heads as Raheem enjoys watching me squirm.

"Thanks, man. We will," Jeremy says, answering for us. I don't know who Raheem's trying to fool with the friend act. He's up to something and I know it. Speaking of acting, Nellie and Chance finally join the rest of us, showing off her new crown.

"Hey, princess," Jeremy says.

"Hey, Jeremy." Nellie stands next to Mickey and Nigel with Chance close by. "You missed it. This must've been the most exciting homecoming yet," she says, checking her head to make sure the petite rhinestone headdress is on straight. I'm sure she won't be seen without that thing for at least a week.

"Oh, yeah, why is that?" Jeremy says, hitting Chance on the arm.

"If you would've been here, you'd know," Nellie says. Even though it's her night, she's still concerned about me in her own way. Hopefully, this is the beginning of her coming down off that high horse she's been on lately.

"Hey, do we have to get into this again? It's over now and you won your crown," Jeremy says, tired of talking about homecoming. Raheem looks bored with the scene as well, or disgusted. Whatever the case, he gestures toward his red Acura Legend coupe, disarming the alarm. I remember when his mom first got that car. Even though it was used, the car was the shit then and still looks good now.

"I'm out. Congrats on the game, man," Raheem says, giving his boy a half hug, the kind brothas give one another, and says his good-byes to the rest of us. "Everyone's invited to the studio tomorrow night. We can consider it a mini celebration for my boy Nigel and you too, Princess Nellie," Raheem says, giving me a sneaky look.

"Later, man," Nigel says, ready to walk Mickey to her car. But, not before Nellie can lay into her.

"Weren't you coming with your man?" Nellie asks Mickey as she and Nigel head toward her car.

"He couldn't make it," Mickey says, giving Nellie an ugly look. I'm glad they're back to normal. Keeping Mickey's secrets is a full-time job.

"So, why are you all hugged up on Nigel?" Nellie says, finally noticing the vibe between Mickey and Nigel. "And what's this about going to the studio? We aren't a bunch of groupies," Nellie says, settling back into herself. Thank God. I can't take the princess act much longer. She's already enough of a diva as it is.

"We're friends," Mickey says. What is it with her and Rah becoming friends with potential lovers? Not that me and Rah are going to be lovers. But, I used to dream about our first time making love back in the day. I had it all planned out, right down to the crushed rose petals on the bed. That's why I know I can't be friends with someone I like. I just don't get it. And neither does Jeremy, I'm sure.

"I hope you have some fun," I say, glad Jeremy decided to come to tonight's session. After running into Raheem last night in the parking lot, I wasn't sure if he really wanted to come. I want to prove to Raheem once and for all that me and Jeremy are the real deal. Maybe then he'll stop trying to hold my hand. I get chills just thinking about his hands touching me and that has got to stop.

"Of course. I need to get to know some of your not school friends, right?" Jeremy says, smiling at me as we head toward Raheem's house. But, something in his smile tells me he knows this is more than a casual session. Mickey's supposed to meet us there. Although she and Nigel are playing it safe by not going out together, I'm still worried about them fooling around. I just don't think it's a good idea. Not only because Mickey's already got a hardcore gangsta as a boyfriend. But also, because knowing about them when Nellie has a crush on Nigel puts me in a difficult position as a friend to them all. I'm just glad Nellie didn't want to come tonight. There's a party at Tania's celebrating her being crowned queen. And, as a princess, Nellie was invited, so you know she ain't missing her chance to be in the popular crowd. Chance accompanied her, even though it isn't really his scene.

When we pull up to the house, Mickey's pink Regal is already parked out front, right behind Nigel's green Impala. Jeremy pulls up behind Nigel's car, commenting on the classic vehicle.

"That's one of the cleanest Impala's I've ever seen," he says, walking over to my side to help me out. "Whose ride is this?" Jeremy says, almost breaking his neck he's looking so hard at the ride.

"Nigel's," I say, leading the way up the sidewalk toward Raheem's house. I didn't want to dress up too much since I'm out with Jeremy, who is always underdressed for my crowd. But, I didn't want to under dress either. Thank God a long skirt, tight T-shirt, and sandals work well for any occasion.

"At least your friends have good taste in cars," he says, eyeing Mickey's car too.

"We may not be able to ball like your friends. But, we can still floss," I say. When we walk up the porch steps toward the already-opened front door, I notice a female I've never seen before in the kitchen playing with Kamal. Who the hell is this?

"Jayd!" Kamal screams, running up to me with a bowl in his hand, giving me my customary hug. "Trish was just giving me some ice cream. Want some?" he asks, offering me a spoonful of his rocky road.

"Nah, 'lil man. I'm cool. And, why are you always trying to feed me?" I say, playing with his mini afro and following him into the kitchen with Jeremy on my tail.

"Maybe he thinks you need to eat," Raheem says, coming in from the studio. As soon as he steps into the kitchen, I feel like the wind's been knocked out of me he looks so good.

"What's up, Jeremy," Rah says, walking over and greeting us both. "This is my girl, Trish," he says, gesturing toward her and looking at me sideways. I knew he had something up his sleeve when he invited us over here tonight. "Trish, this is Jeremy and Jayd." Trish doesn't say anything to us. Instead, she nods her head "what's up" and walks to the studio. Cute and mute, just like he likes his hos.

"What's up, man. Nice place," Jeremy, says, looking around at the Black art on the walls, the flat, screen television and aquarium in the living room. "Nice fish."

"Ah, yeah, man. You know, they soothe me when shit gets rough," Rah says, rubbing his stomach like he's full. "Nigel and Mickey are in the back watching *Scarface*," he says. "If y'all want something to eat we got chicken and waffles from Pann's, peach cobbler, and some drinks in the back," he says as he leads Kamal into the living room to watch a video while Jeremy and I leave the kitchen and enter the studio.

Walking in, our eyes have to adjust to the dim light. But, even a blind person can see Mickey and Nigel making out in the producer's corner. Trish, sitting on one side of the long couch and sipping her drink, is watching *Scarface* like she's never seen it before and bobbing her head to the smooth beat playing in the background. This broad looks like a straight Westingle skank. And, I'm not only saying that because she's here with Raheem and feeding Kamal, which used to be my job. She really does look like an uppity ho: Prada or Gucci black off-the-shoulder dress, black heels with her custom-made hair hanging down to her waist. Her nails are freshly manicured with french tips, and a platinum chain and bracelet to match with diamond studs on her earlobes her Daddy probably bought her for Christmas. This broad reeks Ladera Height's money.

"This is my favorite part," Rah says, entering the room and passing Jeremy and me to sit on the couch, next to the skank.

Jeremy gently pushes against my back, urging me to sit down. And I do, right next to Rah and Jeremy. Shit, the last place I want to be is in between the two of them. But, I can't seem to get out of this one.

"Nigga, come up for air. Here's the best part," Rah says, interrupting Nigel and Mickey's flow. And, he's right. As many times as I've seen this movie on his account, this is our favorite part.

"Hey, Jayd, Jeremy," Mickey says from her comfy spot on Nigel's lap. "When did y'all get here?"

"About two monkey bites ago," I say, laughing at my girl, who looks very happy and unscathed by my response. She looks at Trish and rolls her eyes, indicating she's getting the same vibe from her as I am: another stuck-up, hating broad. Nigel, appearing just as happy as Mickey, looks from me to Jeremy and back to Raheem and smiles, before getting into character.

"Hey, yo, Vinny. Close the shop, man," Nigel and Jeremy mimic in unison, along with the movie.

"Ah, my man's a fan," Rah says, giving Jeremy dap across my lap. Ah, hell no. I got to move, but there's nowhere to go but the floor.

"Jeremy, are you hungry?" I ask, reaching to the table in front of us to grab a waffle. I love Pann's food. Most people around here prefer Roscoe's and it is good. But, Pann's is where it's at for me.

"Nah, I'm good. But, maybe in a little while I'll need to munch," he says, pulling out a bag full of weed from his pocket. "Anybody smoke?" Jeremy asks, passing the bag behind me to Rah.

"Where'd you get this shit?" Rah asks before revealing his own stash. "This almost looks like the strain I slang."

"My homeboy grows it," Jeremy says, taking Rah's stash and inspecting it before passing it back. What homeboy? I wonder. I know Jeremy smokes with his friends, but he's never smoked around me before. Well, except at Matt's. But, even then I've never seen him carry his own stash, until now.

"White boys always have the bomb shit," Rah says, opening Jeremy's bag and smelling the contents. Nigel's eyes peak from across the table, ready to take a whiff. No matter the issue, weed is like the peace pipe around here. Bring your own shit to share and you're as good as in.

"Yes, they do," Nigel says as Mickey takes the bag from Rah and opens it for Nigel to catch a scent of. "I got the blunts," he says, momentarily lifting Mickey off his lap to reach into the desk drawer and retrieving the pack of Swisher Sweet's cigars.

"I can roll," Mickey says enthusiastically. Her man taught her well and gives her plenty of practice. Trish, frowning like she just farted, turns her nose up and rolls her eyes.

"Rah, I thought you said you wasn't smoking blunts no more," Trish says, completely changing the vibe. Al Pacino's on the screen, screaming what Rah looks like he's feeling.

"Trish, I never said that. You said you didn't want me to smoke blunts and I never said anything," he says, reaching across my lap to the table, grabbing a drumstick. I look at Jeremy who's engrossed in the movie and couldn't care less about the drama going down next to me. "Besides, you ain't my mama," he says, obviously irritated with the tone in her voice. If it's one thing Rah doesn't like, it's someone telling him what to do.

"I know that, fool. But them things stink and are so ghetto," she says. As Mickey passes the carefully rolled blunt to Rah, who passes it to Jeremy to light, Mickey gives Trish a look that shuts her mouth right up. She doesn't know a thing about ghetto until Mickey shows her. And, she's lucky Mickey's comfortable. Otherwise, that heffa would be in for a beat-down.

"Ghetto is as ghetto does," Rah says, taking a hit from the blunt Jeremy's just passed over me to him. "Ain't that right, Pacino?" Rah says, acknowledging the television before passing to Nigel, who gives it to Mickey before taking a draw himself. I guess me and Trish are the only two nonsmokers in the room.

"I got papers if you need some," Trish says. So, she does smoke, just not blunts. She probably only smokes a certain brand of papers or some shit like that. This broad's too much for me.

"No, I don't." Why is she talking to me? I don't like being put on the spot. I wonder if she knows about me and Rah's past, unlike Jeremy. It would be just like a heffa to bring up my past with her boyfriend in front of my boyfriend. But luckily, the men are high and ready to socialize, getting the session started their way.

"I don't know anyone who doesn't like *Scarface*," Nigel says, watching the movie while Mickey begins to doze off on his chest. From the looks of it, they're the only happy couple here and they're not even a real couple. I feel so uncomfortable sitting between Jeremy and Rah I haven't even held Jeremy's hand. And, he hasn't reached for mine. I wonder if he feels my unease.

"Yeah, talk about a cult classic," Jeremy says, keeping the rotation going. "This is the reason I started selling in the first place," he says, drawing attention to the fact he also sells weed. Or sold, since he gave it up after he got busted at school a few weeks ago. Now, he's just a faithful consumer.

"You started selling weed because of a movie?" Raheem asks, passing the blunt to Nigel who looks like he's ready for the showdown. Rah's serious about two things: his music and his family. Weed has supported both of them and hustling isn't fun and games to him at all. His dad's in jail behind slanging, his mom's dancing, and he does what he does. Selling weed isn't a hobby to Raheem and he can't stand people who think it is. He's about to go off and now I really want to move.

"Yeah, man," Jeremy continues. "When I saw Tony Montana gaining control of his cash flow by selling drugs, I thought, my dad has it wrong all these years, working hard to get patents and shit and he's miserable," Jeremy says. He must be hella faded because he sounds real stupid right now, even to me. Nigel and Rah are too smart to hustle for long. They see it as a means to an end, not a way to rebel or piss off their parents. It's a whole other hustle out here.

"Your dad's loaded, Jeremy. What are you talking about?" I say, hoping to check him before Rah does. Jeremy may be smart and intelligent in his White boy, atheist kind of way. But, Rah's wise through life experience, books and street hustle: a lethal combination.

"Yeah, but it doesn't make him happy," he says, not picking up the "shut up" tone in my voice. Damn it, I wish he would.

"You White boys are never satisfied," Rah says, relaxed and confident, ready to school Jeremy, whose only shield at the moment is me. And, I'm ready to go in the other room to check on Kamal. Sitting next to Rah is too much. And, my instincts are telling me to grab Jeremy and head out the door. But, it's too late now. "Your dad works his ass off to support you and you sell weed. What the hell kind of bull is that, man?" Here we go.

"Rah, calm down man. It ain't that serious," Nigel says, waking a sleeping Mickey with his deep voice. "White folks are always working hard all their lives for money and end up miserable. That ain't nothing new."

"Yeah, but that don't make it right. And, to say he was in-

spired by my nigga Tony is just insulting." Jeremy, who by
now is feeling the tension rise, tries to alleviate the situation
by explaining his point of view.

"All I meant was Montana found another way to survive,
regardless of his circumstances," Jeremy says, putting the
near-finished blunt in the ashtray on the table, before grabbing a waffle and offering me a bite, which I accept. Rah,
noticing the affection, gets a little jealous, and so does his
mute broad.

"Rah, can you get me something to drink? I'm out of Hennessey," Trish says, dangling her empty glass in front of Raheem, who can see nothing but Jeremy's hand on my thigh
as we lay back on the couch, enjoying our waffle. As if she
said nothing, Rah continues his tirade.

"No, my nigga, no," he says, laughing a little as he does
when he gets really pissed. "Tony Montana is a Cuban refugee
who came to another post–slave society looking to support
himself and his sister. That's it. That was his American dream
and it turned into a nightmare. There was no choice involved,
no daddies with money to run to when shit didn't work out
for him," he says, now on a roll.

"There's always a choice," Jeremy says. As Jeremy talks, a
picture of Rah kissing me flashes into my head. What the
hell?

"Yes, there is." And, as if reading my thoughts again, Rah
touches the side of my thigh, on the low, without missing a
beat. "And, choosing to be a hustler in a shitty ass society not
built for you to survive ain't one of them." And, with that
final comment, I grab Jeremy's arm and say good night.

"Jeremy, I need to get home. I have work tomorrow and
I'm still tired from last night," I say, trying not to be too obvious, but still get Jeremy out of here before Rah really punks
him. "It was nice meeting you Trish, I'll see y'all on Monday,"

I say to Mickey and Nigel who are laughing at the quick turn of events.

"Damn, Jayd, where you going, girl? It's still early," Mickey says, rolling another blunt. "The session's just getting started."

"Yeah, you didn't even get to hear our shit," Nigel says, looking victorious. He's glad Rah got to me tonight. He's always been Rah's personal cheerleader as far as he and I are concerned. No matter how many times Rah hurt me, Nigel was always there defending him.

"Thanks for having us, man, and I'm sorry we didn't get to listen to your demo. My girl's got to get up early. You know how it is," Jeremy says, seemingly unaffected by the tension in the room. That's one thing I love about him: He keeps a cool head no matter what. He takes my hand, ready to go.

"That's alright, man. Some of us hustle at night, some in the day. Besides, I'm sure there will be another time," Rah says, standing up to shake Jeremy's hand before we head out the back door. "Thanks for stopping by, man. I know how precious Jayd's time is," he says, looking my way. Jeremy looks from Raheem to me, knowing something's up.

"Tell Kamal I'll check him later," I say, slamming the door behind me. This was a bad, bad idea.

~ 18 ~
Boy Friends

"You're everything I wanted
Before I knew just what I wanted."

—USHER

"What was all that nonsense about you selling weed because you wanted to be like Scarface?" I say, immediately cutting into him as we walk toward the car. I didn't want to pounce on him fully in front of everyone. But, now that we're alone, Jeremy's got it coming to him.

"I was serious," he says, slowing down to look me in the eye. "Look, when I was growing up, all we ever heard about was the family business and growing wealth, blah, blah, blah. My brothers and I just wanted to surf. As we got older, my mom and dad's marriage started to deteriorate because he was never home and when he was, he drank, which is why my mom started drinking." Well, that explains the preoccupation with champagne at the family dinner I went to with him a few weeks ago. Everybody was lit even before we got there.

"And, what does any of this have to do with Tony Montana?" I ask, not letting him off the hook. As sympathetic as I am toward his alcoholic family, it still has nothing to do with his selling weed. Well, at least not in my opinion. People slang when they need to, not to rebel against their rich families. There are other, more productive ways to do that.

"When my brother Mike came home from college one

year, he took me and Justin to the beach for a midnight surf. It was the first time I'd ever surfed by the moonlight," he says, looking up at the clear sky and a full moon. "His friend's father, who's wealthier than anyone I know, kicked him out for not wanting to go into the family business. So, he started selling weed and ended up very happy, on the beach, with his girl and two kids."

"OK, still not seeing the Scarface connection," I say, unconvinced. He doesn't know I come from a family full of dudes. And, so far, his explanation ain't enough for me.

"When we got home that morning, we slept all day and I watched *Scarface* for the first time with my brothers that night. The story really had an impact on me. Between Tony's ability to come from refugee status to a drug lord—even though it was hardcore drugs and violence and shit I never want any part of—and my brother's friend's ability to defy his family and still be successful and content, I knew I wouldn't follow in my father's footsteps. Even though Mike ended up going into engineering like my dad, he's miserable like him too. Justin and I decided we would take over a different arena, like Scarface, and be happy while doing it."

"That's some serious White boy logic you got going on there, Jeremy," I say, not totally convinced, but I have a better understanding of his thought process now. And, who am I to judge? I remember when Rah came home after his dad was taken to prison and told me he started slanging like his dad. I thought it was the stupidest thing I'd ever heard, especially since he personally experienced the way that life usually ends. But, I didn't judge him. If he saw that as the only way to feed himself and his little brother immediately, I was with him.

"Even though I may not have the financial hardships Raheem thinks necessary to slang, we all want the same thing," he says, putting his arms around my waist and his forehead up against mine, forcing me to feel him, literally.

"And, what's that?" I ask, looking at him. He's too cute for me to stay upset with him for long.

"Freedom," he says, kissing me and making me forget we're outside of Rah's house. After a few minutes of the softest kisses ever, we continue down the driveway toward the car.

"How did you say you know Raheem?" Jeremy asks, opening the car door for me to get in. It's chilly in the car and I just really want to go home. It's been one hell of a week and I'm tired. But, I don't think Jeremy's in any condition to drive me home quite yet. For now, we need to sit in the car and chill until his high comes down. I know how to drive, but I don't have my license yet. So, he's the only designated driver around here. As he gets settled into the driver's seat, I see he has the same thoughts and reclines the seat back to chill for a while.

"We went to junior high together," I say, reclining my seat alongside his to lay back. He only had a couple of hits, so he should be cool in a little while. I'm sure Rah and his crew won't be out for a while, so we should be fine.

"Yeah, but there was more going on in the room than just some regular old junior high buddy shit," he says, closing his eyes, ready for a peaceful slumber. "I may be White, Jayd. But, I'm not clueless," he says, placing his hand on my thigh which has been a hot spot this evening. Maybe too hot.

"Jeremy, I didn't want to tell you that Rah—I mean Raheem—is my ex from way back. It seemed frivolous," I say. Looking at me obviously try to cover my tracks, he smiles and takes my hand from my lap, kissing it softly.

"We all have our pasts. One thing you should know about me is you don't have to lie to me about yours. I'm cool that you were with someone before me," he says, making me feel very stupid. Why did I feel the need to keep the truth from him? It's just like in Maman's story when Jon Paul finds out about her and Pierre's friendship, which she lied about from the start. Maybe if she told him about it in the beginning, he wouldn't have ever felt the need to be jealous. But of course, Jon was crazy and went to extremes to possess Maman. But, the lesson is the same. If you're in a relationship, tell the truth, even when it hurts.

"Yeah, like Tania. You never told me about her," I say as I tightly grasp his hand, hoping to make peace with him. There's something very special about Jeremy and I don't want to scare him away.

"I told you, that was just sex, for both of us," he says, giving me an intense look. "My friendship with her was nothing compared to my relationship with you. Jayd, I love you. I know it's soon and it may catch you a little off guard. But, I've never felt this strongly about anyone before." Sitting up fully, face to face, he says it again. "I love you and I know it. Otherwise, I wouldn't have come to check out the competition," he says, casually lying back down as if he just checked the time.

"So, you knew all along Rah was my ex?" I say, wondering how he found out. But then I guess some things will always remain a secret.

"Let's just say I suspected as much. You seemed pretty tight-lipped about your relationship with Nigel. So, I figured it was either him or Raheem. Then, meeting up with everyone last night was enough to solidify the deal. You were practically screaming without saying a word when he invited me to the session tonight, which is why I decided to come." He's been playing me all along. He's too cool and calm about his shit, never giving up what he's really thinking or feeling. How am I going to read him? Maybe that's the point: I won't be able to.

"Damn, you really are good at chess, aren't you?" I say, realizing he just saw ahead by like five moves. How will I ever hide anything from him? I mean, yeah I should be honest, but not to a fault. Another valuable lesson I've learned from Maman's story is that men can't always handle everything we women can throw at them.

"The best. So, remember that the next time someone tries to steal my queen," he says, pulling me in for a kiss. "So, anymore secrets I should know about?" Oh, nothing more than I come from a long line of voodoo queens and I think I'm still feeling Rah, but not like I'm feeling you. How do I drop all of that on him in one night? Best to leave this discussion for another time.

"No. Anything else I should know about?" Jeremy pauses for a moment, seeming to think about something he wants to reveal. I can see in his luminescent eyes something more. But, rather than full disclosure, he chooses secrecy, which I can respect no matter how hypocritical it may be.

"When there's something to tell, I'll let you know." OK, now that sounds like something a little more than nothing. What the hell is he hiding now? "But, in the meantime, I want to enjoy being with you, Lady J." As we settle in for a couple of hours of chill time, I can't help but wonder what he's hiding now. And furthermore, what Rah's going to do next. Just my luck, I have two excellent chess players trying to seize the queen in me.

After Jeremy drops me off tonight, I stay up a little while longer reading my spirit notebook. I really need to catch up on my writing. But, the few things I've jotted down all have one thing in common: boys. Mama's right. They're at the root of most of my problems, especially with girls. I can see this Mickey and Nellie drama coming, and it's over Nigel, who already has a girlfriend. Same with me and Rah. There's already been tension in my relationship because of a dude who's supposed to be my friend.

But, can boys and girls really be friends? I decide to make that today's conversation topic at work. It's a full crew today, being it's the first Sunday and most Black folks go to church on this Sunday if none other for the entire month, which means our after church lunch crowd will be ridiculous.

"Hell no, boys can't be your friend, Jayd. Look at Alonzo. He's had a crush on you for over a year now and can't get over it. He'll never be your real friend, Jayd," Summer says, dropping knowledge as always.

"I agree with you, Summer," Alonzo chimes in, coming to the front from the kitchen to jump in the conversation. "I could never be your friend and I don't want to," he says, pulling me into him and hugging me tightly. He's hella cool. With long, shiny black hair in fly cornrows and a tattoo of his native Mexico on his forearm, he has all the women that come through here hungry for his fine, short ass.

"Step off, Alonzo. She's got a man or two," Sarah says, trying to be funny. I already briefed her on my date last night.

"Shut up, smart ass. I only have one man," I say, untangling myself from Alonzo's grip. I have to admit, he does gives the best hugs. But, I get the same feeling hugging him as I do when I hug Chance or Nigel, which is nothing compared to the rush I feel when I hug Jeremy or even look at Rah. And, speak of the devil, Kamal and Raheem walk into Simply Wholesome, right on cue.

"Jayd," Kamal says. I walk from behind the counter to give him a big hug.

"He was disappointed you didn't say good night last night," Rah says. "I thought I'd bring him by to tell you himself." Summer, Sarah, and Alonzo look at Rah, already knowing who he is.

"Raheem, these are my coworkers Sarah, Alonzo, and our manager Summer," I say, introducing the curious crew. "This is my friend Raheem and his little brother, Kamal."

"Nice to meet y'all," Rah says.

"I know what you want," I say to Kamal as I go back around the counter to get us each a spinach patty.

"Yes," Kamal exclaims. Satisfied, he goes to the book section to browse as Rah and I step outside to talk.

"So, you break up with the White boy yet?" he asks, assuming his stunt to make Jeremy look stupid worked last night.

"No and I'm not going to," I say. "This is so typical of you, Raheem," I say, referring to last night's session. "Coming back into my life and stirring up all these feelings in me and not telling me you have a girlfriend. This story is so tired. When are you going to grow the hell up and leave me alone?"

"Never, girl. You know that. We made a pledge in the seventh grade to be friends forever. Now, I know those pledges in the dirt behind the bleachers didn't mean much to you," he says, making me smile through my rage. "But, I remembered them all." Just when I think my memories of us kissing would remain just that—incomplete memories, Raheem takes me into his arms and kisses me long and hard. And, although I can hear myself protesting, I don't act on it. Instead, I fully welcome the rise I'm getting from feeling his passion again.

Letting me go, Rah looks at me and smiles. I'm shocked and don't know what to do next. Without hesitation, Rah slowly kisses me again, allowing us to stay locked in each other's arms for what seems like an eternity. Oh, hell no. Now what? I can't wait to get home and tell my mom about this mess. Maybe she'll know what to do.

"Take it from me, men can never be friends with a woman they have feelings for," my mom says as we load the car with my bags. I'll be glad when I don't have to move myself from place to place every week. It's a hassle trying to keep up with my life as it is. It was very busy at work today and I had to write down all of my dreams plus the lessons I learned from Maman's story before getting back to Mama's tonight, not to mention working on my English paper.

"Well, I don't know what to do. I don't want to let go of either one of them. But, Rah just won't get the message." And, I don't know that I want him to. Maybe it's because he was my first kiss and my first love, but I can't seem to shake him. And, after kissing me today, it's going to be a rough road to recovery for me.

"Girl, you better stop this train wreck before it happens. You see what happened to Maman." As we start our trek back to Compton, I can't help but think of all the family heartbreak and tragedy over men. When will this legacy change?

"*With you*," my mom says without actually saying a word. She turns and looks at me, giving me a slight wink.

"Mom," I say, a little frightened of her silent confession. "Have you always been able to read people's minds?" This must be her incarnation of our power.

"Only when people let me. But honestly, this is the first time it's happened since you were born. I always told Mama you took my beauty and my powers. But, the truth is I never developed them. And, that'll change with you, Jayd. Mama sees the future with her sight. Maman saw into people's problems and how to fix them. I can see people's thoughts. And, you. Well, you dream. Until now, that wasn't a part of our legacy. But, then again, neither were brown eyes. You, my little brown-eyed girl, will keep our legacy alive and more powerful than ever before."

"But, how come I never read about your powers in the spirit book?" I ask, when I really mean to say how come she never told me about them.

"I was never allowed to look at the book for long, let alone write in it," she says as we merge from the 110 to the

91, almost home. "Like I told you before, I wasn't at all interested in our heritage, until I needed it for my own good. When I graduated from high school and met your father, I basically cut Mama's weirdness off. Damn, if I'd only known then what I know now," she says, looking regretful. "Listen to Mama, Jayd. Even when you think she's too much, listen to her. Study your lessons. Never turn your sight off."

Although at times I wish I could control my dreams, I'm learning now to accept my destiny. And, with me embracing my gifts, our legacy will live on.

Epilogue

When I get home, Mama is ready and waiting for me in the spirit room. We stay in there all night, grating cocoa butter, me reciting parts of Maman's history from memory and telling Mama the lessons I've learned so far. She also has made me recall all the prayers and recipes I've learned over the last month since school started. I had no idea how much I'd learned until tonight.

Before falling asleep, Mama suggests that Jeremy should come over for coffee and teacakes soon, making me feel even guiltier about kissing Raheem. When did I become a cheating girlfriend? As I drift off to sleep, I immediately fall into a dream.

Jeremy and I are in the mall, relaxing and sipping on our cherry Icees. As we walk toward the front entrance, Jeremy goes to the restroom, leaving me to hold his cup. It's then that I run into Tania, who looks completely different. Time has passed, and she for some reason doesn't attend South Bay High anymore.

"Hey, Jayd," Tania says, acting as if we're old friends. "How's it going?"

"Everything's cool," I say, feeling my hands become numb

from the cold drinks. "How's everything with you?" I ask, feeling extremely uncomfortable. *Jeremy will be out in a minute and I don't want him to see this broad.*

"Oh, everything's fine," she says, putting her left hand in my face for me to see her huge ass diamond engagement ring. "I'm getting married in a few weeks and moving to New York where my husband's law firm is." *Married? She's too young to get married. But, to each her own.*

"Congratulations," I say, feeling relieved. *One less broad to worry about.*

"Oh, and when you see Jeremy, can you tell him to get the adoption papers back to me a soon as possible? It's kind of important," she says like she just asked which way to the MAC counter. "Later."

Frightened by my vision, I awake and sit straight up in my bed. What the hell was that all about? I know Tania has deeper feelings for Jeremy, which are evident in her shameless flirting in front of me. But, this is much, much more. Like my mom and Summer said, dudes and broads can never be solely friends, not if one has it bad for the other. Those are the kinds of friends no one needs.

Drama High, Volume 3:
JAYD'S LEGACY

L. Divine

ABOUT THIS GUIDE

The following questions are intended to
enhance your group's reading of
DRAMA HIGH: JAYD'S LEGACY
by L. Divine.

DISCUSSION QUESTIONS

There's always some drama going on at South Bay High. But that's as it should be. After all, this is Drama High. In this volume, the drama club nominated Nellie as their candidate for homecoming Princess, Jeremy refused to take Jayd to the homecoming dance, and Jayd's old boyfriend—her first love—shows up. That's a lot of drama. Take a moment and consider the following questions to enhance your reading of this power-packed volume of DRAMA HIGH.

1. Did the Drama Club make the right choice in supporting Nellie as their candidate for homecoming Princess? Should they have chosen Jayd instead? Why or why not?

2. Is Raheem a threat to Jayd and Jeremy's relationship? Who do you think she should be with? Should she go back to Raheem or stay with Jeremy? Why or why not?

3. How are Raheem and Jeremy similar? How are they different? Can the two of them be friends?

    (For those of you who've already read DRAMA HIGH: THE FIGHT and DRAMA HIGH: SECOND CHANCE, how different and/or similar is Raheem from KJ? For those of you who haven't read DRAMA HIGH: THE FIGHT or DRAMA HIGH: SECOND CHANCE, go out immediately and catch up on the drama!)

4. Is Jayd changing for Jeremy? If so, in what ways is she changing? Are these changes for the better? If she's not changing, how is she managing to stay the same person she's always been? Is it difficult not to change who you are when you're in a relationship?

5. Should Jeremy have taken Jayd to the homecoming dance? What would you have done in Jayd's place? Would you

have broken up with Jeremy or stayed with him? Did Jayd do the right thing?

6. What are Raheem's and Nigel's opinions on Jayd's relationship with Jeremy? Are they right? Why or why not?

7. Both Mickey and Nigel have significant others. Knowing that, should Mickey have gone to the dance with Nigel? Is there anything wrong with having something on the side?

8. Does Tania want Jeremy back? Will she become a threat to Jayd and Jeremy's relationship? How would you handle the Tania issue in Jayd's place?

9. Chance is stone cold in love with Nellie. Why won't Nellie put him out of his misery and go out with him? Would they make a good match?

10. Tania and Laura stand accused of playing a dirty trick on Nellie to ruin her reputation and ensure she wouldn't win homecoming Princess. How would you have handled the situation? Is more retaliation still owed?

11. What do you think of Jeremy's explanation for selling weed? Is it a good reason or is Jeremy a rich white boy without a clue? Was Raheem right to react the way he did? Is there ever a good reason to sell weed?

12. Did the details of Jayd's legacy and her family history help Jayd in the school drama or did it hinder her?

13. What drama do you think is coming in the next installment of DRAMA HIGH? What would you like to see happen? Pool your ideas together and send them to the author at *www.dramahigh.com.*

Stay tuned for the next book in
the DRAMA HIGH series
FRENEMIES.
Until then, satisfy your DRAMA HIGH craving
with the following excerpt from the next
exciting installment.

ENJOY!

Prologue

"*Sometimes, the people you think are your friends can be worse than enemies,*" my mom says. *I can hear her voice, but I can't see a thing. I feel suspended in time, like I'm in between the dream world and reality.*

"*Yeah, mom. I feel you.*" Did I say that aloud or in my head?

"*They pretend to be your friend while all the time, they really want more. They either want to feed off your popularity, talent, cookies, anything you've got to give. Whatever they think they can have, they will take.*"

This feels too real to be just a dream.

"*Remember Jayd, lust takes and love gives. And, I'm not talking about material things. Friends give their true selves to you. Frenemies, on the other hand, pretend to give until you start reciprocating. Then, the giving turns into taking. And those are not friends. Those people are leaches. And, like all leaches, they must be eliminated in order for you to thrive.*"

For the second time since falling asleep last night, I sit straight up in my bed, breathing hard and sweating like I just ran a mile. Good thing I shower in the morning. Damn, what was that? It wasn't really a dream. It was more like a psychic conversation between me and my mom. I wonder if she did that on purpose.

My mom being able to read my mind still really freaks me out. She says she can only get in my head. Now she's sneaking into my dreams. Man, this is getting to be a bit much for a sistah. But, like my mom said, it comes with the territory of being a Williams woman, just like our never-ending drama.

"Jayd, wake up, girl. You're already five minutes late," Mama says without moving from her comfortable position in the bed across from mine. How she knows what time it is without looking, I'll never know. But, I know she's right. I can hear Bryan stirring around in the kitchen, so I know it must be past time for me to get up. As I stumble out my twin sized bed to retrieve my outfit for the day from the back of the bedroom door, I accidentally step on the rhinestone sandals Jeremy bought me; it's sticking out from underneath my bed.

"Remember your mother's words Jayd," Mama says, making me recall the dream I just snapped out of. As if it isn't bad enough that I have Mama in my head, now my mom has crept her way in, too. What the hell?

~ 1 ~
Just Friends

"You, you got what I need/
But you say he's just a friend."

—BIZ MARKIE

After both Rah's surprise kiss yesterday afternoon and my first dream last night about Jeremy being Tania's baby-daddy, I'm even more confused about what to do with Rah and Jeremy. I can't front; Rah's kiss is still making me tingle and I have to see Jeremy this morning. How can I look Jeremy in the eyes after what I did? Well, technically, what Rah did. But I could have stopped him, if I really wanted to.

"Jayd, get out the bathroom. I need to go, now," my cousin Jay says, snapping me back into my morning routine. My cornrows are shiny from the mint shea butter Mama and I made last night. Mama supplies most of the beauty products for Netta's Never Nappy Beauty shop: hair oil, sprays, lotions, soaps, essential oils, you name it. If it can be made, Mama can make it. And, it'll be ten times better than anything you can buy at the beauty supply store.

"Give me one more minute and then the bathroom's all yours," I say, packing up my toiletries into my bath towel before taking one more look in the mirror. My yellow Africa 1 T-shirt goes perfectly with my complexion, making my spirits lift. I love wearing bright colors. They make me feel good, despite whatever shit in my environment may be coming my way.

"I don't have a minute, girl. Get out, now!" Jay can be such a drama queen sometimes, I swear.

"Go around back and let it out. You a dude," I say as I continue to primp in the mirror. My uncles and Jay—probably Daddy, too— have all taken a piss out back before either out of necessity or some sort of male bonding thing. It ain't nothing new to him.

"It ain't like that Jayd," Jay says, almost groaning. I guess I better let him in. Man, I miss the semi-privacy of my mom's house on the weekends. At least I don't have to share the bathroom with a bunch of men while I'm there. But, it's only Monday, which means I have a entire week before I get some privacy again.

After returning my bathroom necessities to one of my three garbage bags turned dresser drawers in Daddy's room, I head to the kitchen to find Bryan eating breakfast and ready to go to work up the street at Miracle Market. He didn't get in until hella late last night and I'm surprised to see him up and alert, even though his eyes are beet red.

"Hey Jayd," Bryan says in between mouthfuls of corn-flakes. I'm sure it's his second or third bowl. Early morning munchies can do that to a brotha.

"What's up? Glad you made it home this morning," I say, grabbing a banana from the kitchen counter, heading into the dining room to retrieve my backpack and put on my sandals before heading out the door. I pull my sweater off the back of the chair where my purse is sitting and slip it on even though it's going to be a warm day. It's October and the weather is finally changing. And I'm sure it'll be even cooler once I get to Redondo Beach.

"Don't hate because Mama keeps you on lock down, Blackerella," he says, thinking his little joke is funny. But, it's not, and I'm tired of the double-standard around here. If I'm supposed to be from a long line of powerful women, how come it seems we have so many limitations? Why can't I hang till late like Bryan?

"Whatever," I say, tired of this argument. "I got to go before I miss my bus," I say, opening the heavy door before tackling with the security gate. The wrought-iron has been bent for years, making it hard to open.

"Wait up. I'll walk with you," Bryan says as he steps in front of me to open the gate in one quick motion. "Upper body strength: another perk of being a man." As he steps back into the kitchen to grab his bag, I step outside on the front porch and take in a breath of fresh morning air. I love this time of the morning. Everything feels clean before the dew melts. Bryan slides his black bag over his head, barely missing his dreads.

"When you gone twist your hair up," I ask. He looks like a poodle before it gets its hair cut. And, his hair growis fast.

"As soon as I find somebody I can trust to twist it up for me," he says, nudging me as we walk down the street toward Alondra Boulevard. He's been trying to get me to do his hair for a while now. But, I ain't looking forward to the charity work.

"You know a sistah don't work for free," I say, nudging him back, but harder.

"How you gone make a nigga pay and we blood," he says, looking genuinely hurt.

"How you gone expect something for free and we blood," I say, mimicking his pitch perfectly. Bryan is more like a brother to me and I love him the most out of all my uncles. But, he's cheap, just like my ex KJ. Maybe that's why they can hang. As if he's in my head too, Bryan asks me about the dudes in my life.

"So, how's the White boy? I still can't believe you picked him over KJ," he says, sounding as confused as I feel.

"He's cool," I say looking down at my yellow Bebe sandals. The shiny rhinestones shimmer in the morning sun, making me remember what Rah said about dudes buying me things. Between his warning at Homecoming and my mom's warning in my dream, I'm starting to wonder about Jeremy's true intentions.

"Alright, what's wrong," Bryan says, knowing I'm not telling the whole truth. Damn he's intuitive for a dude.

"Well, Rah kinda came back into the picture recently," I say, not wanting to tell him everything that happened. He and Rah used to hang out, but not as much as he and KJ do. Rah was all about spending time with me when he came over, which was pretty much everyday when we were together. It was who he hung with after he left my house that was the problem.

"Rah? What's that nigga up to? Him and Nigel still hanging tight," he asks.

"Yeah, Nigel goes to South Bay now," I say. I still can't believe it myself. How did my world get so small?

"Fo' sho'? That's some good shit right there. Now I won't be so worried about your ass," he says, pushing me off the curb as we approach Miracle Market.

"Glad my social life meets with your approval," I say, a little saltier than necessary. But, this male bonding shit really gets on my nerves sometimes.

"What's got your panties all up in a bunch," he says, taking out a spliff and lighting it right in front of the store. Bryan has no fear.

"Without getting too detailed, Rah says he just wants to be friends but I don't think he's telling the whole truth," I say, leaving out the juicy kiss he planted on me.

"He's probably not, Jayd and you know that. So, what's the problem?"

"The problem is I just got into a new relationship and there's already so much drama."

"Well maybe it's the universe's way of telling you to make a different choice." If street philosophy was a major in college, Bryan would have a PhD. in the shit.

"Oh, here you go. You need to apply for a job as a therapist or something and stop wasting your time working at the Miracle Mart," I say as I walk away from his cannabis cloud, toward the bus stop on the corner.

"No thanks. I like my life just the way it is," Bryan says as he takes one last draw before putting it out and back into his bag, ready for work. "Can you say the same thing?"

As the bus pulls up to take me to my first stop in Gardena, I can't help but think about what Bryan just said. What if all this chaos in my relationship with Jeremy is telling me to make a different choice? Then, what do I do?

After last week's Homecoming hype, I'm looking forward to a normal day at school. Nellie gets to sport her new crown around campus all day and I'm glad for my girl. With the lunch procession of the Homecoming court taking up all of her time, we probably won't get to chill too much today. Even though her head's still in the clouds, I'm glad she's coming down a little.

I can't stop thinking about my dream last night. And, from my experiences, they usually come true in one way or another. I wonder if Tania really is pregnant with Jeremy's child. Wouldn't that be some shit? Young Middle Eastern girls getting married ain't really all that surprising around here. But, one of them being pregnant by a White boy would certainly make heads turn, I'm sure. Speaking of which, here's my White boy now.

"Hey baby," Jeremy says as he reaches across the passenger's seat, taking my backpack and throwing it into the back-seat while I sit down for the short ride up the hill to campus. If South Bay High didn't have so much drama, it wouldn't be such a foul place to come to every day. It's a clear morning and the unobstructed view of the ocean is always refreshing.

"Hey Jeremy," I say as we kiss. I haven't spoken to him since early yesterday afternoon. I stayed up all night with Mama working in the spirit room and didn't get a chance to call him before I went to sleep. All I can think about now is Raheem's lips touching mine. What the hell?

"How was your evening, Lady J," he says, pulling his Mustang away from the bus stop and joining the rest of the caravan rushing to get a good parking space. "I called you but I figured you were tired from work." If he only knew the half of it.

"It was fine. Just hella busy. I had a lot of homework to do last night," I say, leaving out the spirit work part of my evening. I don't think I'll ever be able to share that side of my life with him especially since he doesn't believe in God or anything close to it. If I tell him about my lineage as a Voodoo Queen, he'll probably react like Misty and think I'm trying to cast a spell on him. And to think, the first potion I made was to help keep his ass out of jail.

"I hear you. I'm still making up work from my suspension weeks ago. The teachers up here are relentless." Yes, they are, especially when it comes to homework. You'd think we were in college already.

"*I gotta shake it off . . .*" Mariah sings, announcing a phone call. I have to switch up my ringtone every now and then to suit my mood. The caller ID reveals Rah's name, making me tingle just like I did when he kissed me yesterday. This isn't good.

"Hey, can you drop me off right here," I say as we approach the front gate, still in line behind at least twenty other fancy cars waiting to get into the crowded parking lot. "I need to get something out of my locker before the bell rings," I say, only telling half the truth. I just want some space to think for a little while before the day begins.

"Sure thing, Lady J." God, Jeremy's so sweet, making me feel even guiltier about Rah. When did I become the bad one? "I'll catch up with you at break," he says, leaning over to give me a kiss. His lips are so soft and pleasant. I can't hurt him. I just can't.

START YOUR OWN BOOK CLUB

Courtesy of the DRAMA HIGH series

ABOUT THIS GUIDE

The following is intended to help you get
the Book Club you've always wanted
up and running!
Enjoy!

Start Your Own Book Club

A Book Club is not only a great way to make friends, but it is also a fun and safe environment for you to express your views and opinions on everything from fashion to teen pregnancy. A Teen Book Club can also become a forum or venue to air grievances and plan remedies for problems.

The People

To start, all you need is yourself and at least one other person. There's no criteria for who this person or persons should be other than having a desire to read and a commitment to discuss things during a certain time frame.

The Rules

Just as in Jayd's life, sometimes even Book Club discussions can be filled with much drama. People tend to disagree with each other, cut each other off when speaking, and take criticism personally. So, there should be some ground rules:

1. Do not attack people for their ideas or opinions.
2. When you disagree with a book club member on a point, disagree respectfully. This means that you do not denigrate other people for their ideas or even their ideas, themselves, i.e., no name calling or saying, "That's stupid!" Instead, say, "I can respect your position, however, I feel differently."
3. Back up your opinions with concrete evidence, either from the book in question or life in general.
4. Allow every one a turn to comment.
5. Do not cut a member off when the person is speaking. Respectfully wait your turn.
6. Critique only the idea (and do so responsibly; saying, "That's stupid!" is not allowed). Do not criticize the person.

7. Every member must agree to and abide by the ground rules.

Feel free to add any other ground rules you think might be necessary.

The Meeting Place

Once you've decided on members, and agreed to the ground rules, you should decide on a place to meet. This could be the local library, the school library, your favorite restaurant, a bookstore, or a member's home. Remember, though, if you decide to hold your sessions at a member's home, the location should rotate to another member's home for the next session. It's also polite for guests to bring treats when attending a Book Club meeting at a member's home. If you choose to hold your meetings in a public place, always remember to ask the permission of the librarian or store manager. If you decide to hold your meetings in a local bookstore, ask the manager to post a flyer in the window announcing the Book Club to attract more members if you so desire.

Timing is Everything

Teenagers of today are all much busier than teenagers of the past. You're probably thinking, "Between chorus rehearsals, the Drama Club, and oh yeah, my job, when will I ever have time to read another book that doesn't feature Romeo and Juliet!" Well, there's always time, if it's time well-planned and time planned ahead. You and your Book Club can decide to meet as often or as little as is appropriate for your bustling schedules. *Once a month* is a favorite option. *Sleepover Book Club* meetings—if you're open to excluding one gender—is also a favorite option. And in this day of high-tech, savvy teens, *Internet Discussion Groups* are also an appealing option. Just choose what's right for you!

Well, you've got the people, the ground rules, the place, and the time. All you need now is a book!

The Book

Choosing a book is the most fun. THE FIGHT is of course an excellent choice, and since it's a series, you won't soon run out of books to read and discuss. Your Book Club can also have comparative discussions as you compare the first book, THE FIGHT, to the second, SECOND CHANCE, and so on.

But depending upon your reading appetite, you may want to veer outside of the Drama High series. That's okay. There are plenty of options, many of which you will be able to find under the Dafina Books for Young Readers Program in the coming months.

But don't be afraid to mix it up. Nonfiction is just as good as fiction and a fun way to learn about from where we came without just using a history text book. Science fiction and fantasy can be fun, too!

And always, always research the author. You might find the author has a website where you can post your Book Club's questions or comments. The author may even have an e-mail address available so you can correspond directly. Authors will also sit in on your Book Club meetings, either in person, or on the phone, and this can be a fun way to discuss the book as well!

The Discussion

Every good Book Club discussion starts with questions. THE FIGHT, as will every book in the Drama High series, comes along with a Reading Group Guide for your convenience, though of course, it's fine to make up your own. Here are some sample questions to get started:

1. What's this book all about anyway?
2. Who are the characters? Do we like them? Do they remind us of real people?
3. Was the story interesting? Were real issues of concern to you examined?
4. Were there details that didn't quite work for you or ring true?
5. Did the author create a believable environment—one that you could visualize?
6. Was the ending satisfying?
7. Would you read another book from this author?

Record Keeper

It's generally a good idea to have someone keep track of the books you read. Often libraries and schools will hold reading drives where you're rewarded for having read a certain number of books in a certain time period. Perhaps, a pizza party awaits!

Get Your Teachers and Parents Involved

Teachers and Parents love it when kids get together and read. So involve your teachers and parents. Your Book Club may read a particular book where it would help to have an adult's perspective as part of the discussion. Teachers may also be able to include what you're doing as a Book Club in the classroom curriculum. That way books you love to read such as the Drama High ones can find a place in your classroom alongside the books you don't love to read so much.

Resources

To find some new favorite writers, check out the following resources. Happy reading!

Young Adult Library Services Association
http://www.ala.org/ala/yalsa/yalsa.htm

Carnegie Library of Pittsburgh
Hip-Hop!
Teen Rap Titles
http://www.carnegielibrary.org/teens/read/booklists/teen-rap.html

TeensPoint.org
What Teens Are Reading?
http://www.teenspoint.org/reading_matters/book_list.asp?sort=5&list=274

Teenreads.com
http://www.teenreads.com/

Sacramento Public Library
Fantasy Reading for Kids
http://www.saclibrary.org/teens/fantasy.html

Book Divas
http://www.bookdivas.com/

Meg Cabot Book Club
http://www.megcabotbookclub.com/

BOWIE HIGH SCHOOL
LIBRARY MEDIA CENTER